The Quake demon █████████
again, knocking him to ████████
locked around his left wrist. ███████
his right shoulder.

A shockwave rippled between the two points, slamming up his arm and across his chest. He could feel his bones begin to hum as his muscles convulsed. In another moment his teeth would explode like firecrackers. . . .

His right arm was still free. He reached up and grabbed the demon's wrist, wrenching its claw loose from its grip on Angel's shoulder. Now he had it by one wrist and it had him by the other.

Angel put every ounce of strength into a lunge to the side. He took the demon with him—and both its rocky paws plunged into the soft earth of the tunnel.

Angel's body stopped shaking itself apart, and the ground began to shudder instead. Something Angel had learned over the years was that it was generally a lot harder to turn off a mystical source of energy than it was to turn it on . . . and whatever force the demon was generating probably had a much greater affinity for rock and earth than undead flesh.

He was still congratulating himself on his ingenuity when the tunnel collapsed.

Angel™

City Of
Not Forgotten
Redemption
Close to the Ground
Shakedown

Available from POCKET PULSE

ANGEL™

shakedown

Don DeBrandt

**An original novel based on the television series
created by Joss Whedon & David Greenwalt**

POCKET PULSE

New York   London   Toronto   Sydney   Singapore

Historian's Note: This story takes place during the first season of *Angel*.

An *Original* Publication of POCKET BOOKS

 POCKET PULSE published by
Pocket Books, a division of Simon & Schuster, Inc.
1230 Avenue of the Americas, New York, NY 10020

™ and © 2000 by Twentieth Century Fox Film Corporation.
All rights reserved.

ISBN: 0-7434-0696-6

First Pocket Books printing November 2000

10 9 8 7 6 5 4 3 2 1

POCKET PULSE and colophon are registered trademarks of Simon & Schuster, Inc.

Printed in the U.S.A.

Dedicated to my partner Andrea, a fiery Irish lass and the biggest Doyle fan I know. This one's for you, darlin'.

Acknowledgments

I'd like to thank my agent, Lucienne Diver of Spectrum, for all her hard work; my editor, Lisa Clancy, for insightful input; Pauline, who lent me all her *Angel* tapes; and the friends who came to my rescue at the eleventh hour when my computer died and I was a week away from my deadline—Marilyn, Kathleen, John, Steve, and especially the Brick, who analyzed, improvised and overcame.

ANGEL™

shakedown

CHAPTER ONE

Visions suck, Doyle thought.

It's not so much the blinding headaches, the Irishman mused as Cordelia pressed a bag of ice to his forehead. *Or even the sense of impending doom that always goes with 'em. But flailin' about like I've got a chicken stuffed down my pants, in front of Cordy—man, that's just not fair.*

"So, what is it this time?" Cordelia sighed. "Vampires? Werewolves? People who still like disco?"

"Worse," Doyle said, wincing. "Y'know, for a vampire's office this place has entirely too many reflective surfaces." There were glass panels between the inner office and the outer, and it felt like every one of them was sending sharp little glints of light directly into Doyle's skull. At least the window in Angel's office was bricked over.

He closed his eyes and said, "I don't want t'seem overly melodramatic, but I think I just saw the whole city get destroyed."

"Tell us," Angel said.

Doyle opened his eyes and looked over at his boss. Angel sat behind his desk, polishing the head of a Celtic war ax. He looked like he should be wearing blue body paint and a kilt instead of a black silk shirt and pants, lit by a hillside campfire instead of an office lamp.

"What I could really use," Doyle said, taking the ice bag from Cordelia, "is some whiskey and a glass to go with this ice."

"Make with the four-one-one already," Cordelia said. "I mean, is this like Bruce Willis summer blockbuster bad, or Hulk Hogan direct-to-video bad? You know, in terms of special effects."

Doyle's eyes flickered back to Cordelia. She wore a simple summer dress of pale green, probably a knock-off of a more expensive designer label she'd picked up in a thrift store on Melrose. On her, of course, it looked like an original. What Cordy lacked in funds she made up for in attitude.

"Right," Doyle said. "Well, I'd have t'go with door number one. I'm talkin' total city-wide destruction here."

"How?" Angel asked.

"Every L.A. resident's worst nightmare," Doyle answered. "Besides the Olsen twins, o'course. An earthquake. The Big One . . ."

If there was one thing Angel could change about his job, it would be his relationship with The Powers That Be.

The Powers That Be. You could just hear the capital letters when you said it. Angel wondered if their close friends called them The, or maybe TP.

Probably not.

It wasn't that he resented being their instrument. In the great buffet of existence, Angel's plate held a big heaping serving of guilt, liberally sprinkled with regret and remorse. That was seconds; his first helping had consisted mainly of torture, murder, and the occasional maiming. He had a lot to make up for, and he was happy to do it by acting as an agent for a higher power. Doyle got the visions, and Angel did his best to do something about them.

But did they have to be so damn *vague* all the time?

" 'Angel, here's the address and a recent photo of a demon serial killer. Go get him,' " Angel muttered to himself. "That'd be nice. Or maybe, 'Here's a schedule of ritual sacrifices you have to stop, cross-indexed and alphabetized.' *That* would be helpful. What do I get instead? A description of a Universal

3

Studios theme ride and the name of an apartment building."

He was standing in the shadows of a hibiscus bush across the street from the aforementioned building. APPLETREE ESTATES read the sign over the front door. It looked like a fairly new structure, a low-rise spread out over the better part of a block, with an eight-foot stone wall around the perimeter of the grounds. Underground parking, security gates, probably an outdoor pool. Nothing unusual for this part of L.A., a residential neighborhood called Silverlake.

He'd been watching the front door since nightfall, watching people come and go. He was pretty sure he hadn't been spotted so far—"Professional Lurker" was second from the top of Angel's resume, right between "Vampire With a Soul" and "Private Detective Without a License."

And then he saw the demon.

The demon looked normal, for this part of L.A.: thirty-something, handsome, the best hair and teeth money could buy. Custom-tailored suit in a tasteful shade of teal—going out to a dinner meeting with a few studio execs, maybe. The demon paused in the darkening twilight, taking a few deep breaths of air and obviously savoring them. He smiled.

And a slender, forked tongue darted out between his lips.

Anyone else might have missed it, but Angel knew what he'd seen. "Gotcha," he whispered. "Couldn't resist getting a little taste of that delicious L.A. smog, could you? . . ."

A silver Porsche 928 rolled up a moment later and the demon got in. The car drove off.

Angel considered the situation. That tongue had given him an idea; he pulled out his cell phone and made a call.

Twenty-seven minutes later another car pulled up, this one an old white Dodge. Angel walked up to the driver's side.

"Large pepperoni mushrooms?" Angel said, pulling out his wallet.

"You mus' be hungry," the young Latino behind the wheel said. "Mos' people wait 'til I get to the door."

"And I'll give you another twenty for the hat," Angel said.

The driver hesitated, then shrugged and handed over his baseball cap with the pizza chain's logo on it. "Okay by me."

"Uh—there's no garlic on this, right?"

He breezed through the door, going in at the same moment someone else was going out, and didn't get a second glance. The only thing people noticed—or remembered—about someone delivering pizza was the smell.

Apartment buildings were public spaces; as a vampire, Angel had no trouble entering them. For individual dwellings he needed an actual invitation to cross the threshold, but he didn't think that would be a problem. He was only here to do some looking around, get a sense of the place.

So that's what he did. The lobby was undistinguished: a fake fireplace with a plaster mantelpiece, covered with junk mail people hadn't bothered to pick up. A bank of chromed mailboxes, a few potted plants. He roamed up and down the halls, only running into people once or twice and never making eye contact.

He found nothing.

No mysterious sounds from behind locked doors. No pentagrams woven into the carpet. No stench of evil from the laundry room. Just a box full of congealing cheese in one hand and a cap that made him look ridiculous.

"Earthquake," he murmured. "Underground?"

He went down to the parking garage and looked around; nothing but oil stains and vehicles. Maybe he wasn't looking deep enough . . .

He slid the pizza box under a BMW and stuffed the cap into the pocket of his black trenchcoat, then approached the elevator doors on the parking level. There didn't seem to be anybody around.

Angel forced his fingers into the crack of the doors, then used his considerable strength to pry them open. He stuck his head into the elevator shaft and looked down.

This was supposed to be the bottom floor, but the shaft kept going. He couldn't tell how far.

"Well, well," Angel said softly. "And what are we keeping in the basement?"

There were iron rungs set into the side of the shaft for maintenance access. Angel grabbed hold of the nearest one and started climbing down.

He moved quickly, not wanting to get caught by a descending elevator, and reached the bottom, five stories down, within moments. Hoping there was no one on the other side, he pried the doors open on the lowest level.

The hallway he stepped into was similar to the ones on the upper floors, but Angel could tell at a glance that more money had gone into the furnishings. The lighting sconces were cut crystal, the carpet a deep emerald shag with an intricate Celtic knotwork design, the walls done in an expensive *faux* finish with teak trim. Oak-paneled doors lined the corridor. Even the elevator doors were covered with ornate antique brass; it gave Angel something to grip as he forced them closed again.

Just in time. He heard another door open down the hallway as he turned around.

The man who walked out could have been a brother to the demon Angel had first seen, or at least a cousin; he had the same kind of generic good looks all too common to L.A. He was dressed in tennis whites, in stark contrast to Angel's black leather trenchcoat.

They looked at each other for a second. The demon smiled with even white teeth.

The perfect cover story came to Angel in a flash. It was so good, so believable, that the grin he gave the demon in return was completely natural. The reason Angel would give for being there would not only be accepted without question, it would probably net him more information than he needed.

And just as he opened his mouth, the earthquake hit.

The demon grabbed the door frame and hung on, terror on his face. Plaster dust sprinkled down from the ceiling. Doors opened up and down the hallway, other frightened people assuming the same protected position in their doorways.

Frightened people with forked tongues flickering nervously between their lips.

The tremor lasted less than a minute. Angel had been through worse—but he'd been around for a few hundred years. Even so, the prospect of being buried under several tons of rubble was enough to make even a vampire uneasy.

Then it was over, and everyone was asking everyone else if they were okay. Angel's presence wasn't questioned, for which he was thankful but slightly annoyed. It had been such a *good* cover story. . . .

"Everyone all right? Nobody hurt?" asked a tall man striding down the hall. He was dressed in casual clothes, tan slacks and a yellow cotton shirt, but had an air of authority that didn't require a uniform to confirm it. He appeared to be around sixty, with silver hair and the kind of weathered good looks that old movie stars develop.

"We're all right, Galvin," a young woman in shorts and a halter-top said. "A few of the kids are shaken up."

"I think it's time we had a meeting, don't you?" Galvin said. He had the faintest trace of an Irish accent; if Angel hadn't been born on the Emerald Isle himself he wouldn't have noticed.

"Everyone," Galvin said. "In the common room, in ten minutes."

It wasn't hard to tag along and find a seat at the back. The room itself was able to seat around a hundred people, and it was filled to capacity. All the faces were young and handsome; Galvin seemed to be the only senior citizen there. Rows of chairs faced an elaborately carved antique podium at the front—Sotheby's would have listed a starting bid for it at a minimum of ten thousand.

Galvin stood behind the podium. He rapped an equally ancient gavel three times, bringing the meeting to order.

"Well now," he said. His voice was a deep, rich tenor that didn't need a microphone to carry. "This is the third tremor in three days, ever since the original incident. Each one has been stronger than the last. If this continues, they'll bring our house down around our ears."

A man in the second row held up his hand. From where Angel sat, all he could see was the back of an expensive haircut and the Rolex on his wrist. "Can't we negotiate with them?"

Galvin smiled and gave a rueful little chuckle. "Well, if anybody could, you'd think *we* could, right?" Nervous laughter from the crowd. "But this isn't a negotiation. It's a siege. We're in their way, and they plan to be rid of us."

A young woman in a Versace suit spoke up. "Can't we make them an offer? Surely we have something they want."

"We do," Galvin said. "Unfortunately, what we have they've decided to simply take. We're very adept at *finding* leverage, but all the leverage in the world does us no good without the muscle to move the lever. We're wheelers and dealers, not fighters."

Angel got to his feet. "Excuse me," he said. People turned to look at him.

"If you're not fighters," Angel said, "maybe you should think about hiring some."

"Angel," Galvin said. "The vampire with a soul . . ."

Galvin had invited Angel back to his office to talk. The office was as elegant and refined as royalty: polished mahogany paneling, Persian rug over a hardwood floor, a writing desk that had probably come from a French court. The two paintings that hung on the wall could have paid Angel's rent for a century.

"So you've heard of me," Angel said. "I'm afraid I can't say the same about you."

"That's understandable," Galvin said. "We're rather secretive. We like to keep to ourselves—but we're not evil. Brandy?"

"No, thanks. If I'm going to be working for you—"

"—you're going to need to know a little about us, of course. Well." Galvin poured a shot of brandy from an ornate decanter into a snifter. He swirled the liquor around a few times, then let his forked tongue flick out over the top of the glass. "Ah. Sure you won't try some? It's the very best, I assure you."

"I believe you," Angel said. "But that's not what I'm interested in."

"Yes, of course. I'm sorry—it's just that a lifetime

of hiding in the shadows makes it hard to reveal our secrets to an outsider. But we do need your help . . .

"We're called the Serpentene. Just as vampires are demons that have taken over a human body, we're demons that originally took over the bodies of snakes. Over time, we've transformed—shed our skin, so to speak—as a matter of survival. Humanity has an inbred aversion to snakes—not to mention demons—so we've learned to hide our true nature from them."

"You seem to have done pretty well for a group of outcasts."

"Financially, you mean? Oh, yes. The Serpentene are natural deal-makers; we dabble in everything from stock trading to car dealerships. The only thing that limits us is the same problem you have."

"A liquid diet?"

Galvin laughed. "No. Unlike ordinary snakes, our demon heritage makes us nocturnal; we don't like the sun any more than you do."

"Which is why you live underground."

"More or less. We don't burst into flames at the touch of daylight, but we do get sluggish and sleepy. Not very good for business—and we like to spend money."

"I can see that."

"As we've become more human in appearance, we've become more human in nature. We've developed human tastes, especially for the finer things in life. Clothes, cars, furnishings, food and drink; we seek out the best available . . . and that's why we want to hire you."

"To protect you," Angel said. "From whom?"

"Perhaps I should show you," Galvin said, getting up. "Please, come with me."

He led Angel out of the office and down the hall. He stopped in front of a door marked 245 and knocked gently. "Maureen? It's Galvin."

A pretty young redhead with a spray of freckles across her nose opened the door; Angel guessed that Cordelia would have gladly traded her left arm for the woman's dress. "Yes, Galvin?"

"This is Angel. He's going to help us with our problem."

"Oh, yes. I saw you at the meeting."

"I hope I can help," Angel said.

"Maureen, I was wondering if we could see Suzy," said Galvin. "If you think she's up to it."

"She's the same as before," Maureen sighed. "Come on in."

She led them through a living room decorated in black and white—black leather couch and chairs, black metal coffee table, white rug and walls—and down a hall to the bedroom suite.

The large canopy bed was empty—but then Angel heard something move in the corner. He went to investigate the bathroom, by the sunken marble bathtub.

Actually, the noise came from within the tub. From the thing resting inside.

It had once been a woman, or at least female. What it was now was a human-shaped puddle of flesh, like a blow-up doll half-filled with Jell-O. Only the eyes and lips, floating on the surface of the face like lost Mr. Potato-Head accessories, gave any indication the creature was a living thing. It blinked at him slowly, then tried to form words with its toothless mouth. "Hhhhh—ohhhh . . ."

"Suzy, this is Angel," Galvin said softly. "He's going to protect us from what attacked you."

"Gggguhhh . . ."

Angel drew back. "What happened to her?" he whispered.

"A demon assaulted her, last week. She fought back. Even though she was no match for her attacker, I think she managed to anger it. Witnesses said it grabbed both of her wrists, and then she started to . . . shake. Violently. It passed some kind of shockwave through her, one that shattered every bone in her body. Her teeth and fingernails actually exploded."

"Why isn't she—"

"Dead? A human would be. But snakes have always been blessed with a certain . . . *flexibility*. It allowed her to survive."

"Well," said Angel, unable to meet the eyes of the thing in the tub. "Isn't she lucky . . ."

"This is where the attack took place," Galvin said. It was a large office space, irregular rows of desks scattered throughout, each with its own computer and a well-dressed Serpentene behind it. All the office workers wore telephone headsets, and every one seemed to be in the middle of an animated conversation.

"Our sales force, working late as usual," Galvin said. "Since we prefer to stay inside during business hours, we rely heavily on telemarketing."

"I thought you said you weren't evil . . ."

Galvin grinned but didn't reply. He led Angel through the maze of desks to the far wall, his salespeople nodding or waving as they strolled past.

The wall had a sheet of plywood nailed to it, and several planks over the top of that. Angel guessed it was covering up a large hole.

"This is where it came through, last week."

"And what, exactly, was it?"

"A Quake demon."

"Don't think I'm familiar with that breed."

"I'm not surprised. They're completely subterranean, never show their faces aboveground," Galvin said, shaking his head. "Nasty buggers, though. Short, muscular, skin that looks like chunks of raw coal."

"So why are they bothering you?"

"We're not sure. It may be territorial, or have something to do with their religious beliefs. All that's clear is they want us gone—and if they can't terrorize us into moving, they'll turn our home into ruins."

"And maybe the rest of L.A. with it," Angel mused. "All right. Here's what I'm going to do." He pulled a business card out of his pocket and handed it to Galvin. "That's the number of my associates. If I'm not back or you don't hear from me in three hours, call them and let them know the situation." Angel grabbed hold of one of the planks blocking the opening and ripped it off.

"What are you planning?"

Angel pulled another board free. "Oh, you know—go for a stroll, see the sights, do a little spelunking. I'm a big tunnel fan, myself . . ."

The tunnel was bare, packed earth, just tall enough for Angel to stand without stooping. It led downward at a steep angle, and Angel had been following it for half a mile.

"Great," he muttered under his breath. "I've been hired by demon yuppies to fight the Mole Men . . ."

The Mag-lite he was using showed him a branch in the tunnel ahead. "Decisions, decisions . . ."

He took the one on the right and kept going. Since coming to L.A., Angel had spent a lot of time underground; the extensive tunnel system under the city was how he got around during the day. Fortunately, he had a well-developed sense of direction and rarely got lost.

At least not in the physical sense. But being all alone in the dark, the smell of raw earth in his nose, had a way of bringing back memories. Memories of being lost in a different, much deeper way.

Lost in bloodlust, and insanity.

It was 1755, two years after Darla had turned him. Two years of random slaughter across the face of Europe, cutting a swath of blood-drenched decadence. It was the same year a great earthquake rocked Portugal, mocking the efforts of Angelus and his sire with a death toll of thirty thousand. They had been in Madrid, close enough to feel the edge of the shockwave, and when they heard the extent of the disaster they decided to investigate the devastation firsthand as a sort of holiday.

They hired a barge at Aranjuez and floated down the Tagus River, the dark bulk of mountains blotting out the stars on either side of them as they drifted through the Mediterranean night. In two days they reached Lisbon, on the Atlantic coast; once the jewel of the Iberian Peninsula, it was now a vision of Hell. Flames raged unchecked for the fifth day in a row, streets choked with rubble making firefighting impossible. The downtown area, from St. Paul's quarter to St. Roch, was gutted. The Royal Palace and the Opera House were burned-out husks. The rats had already begun to feast on the dead.

The barge crew, hardened men all, were stunned into silence by the destruction. Angelus and Darla raised champagne glasses to toast the spectacle— then ripped out the throats of the crew to fill them.

They'd played in the ruins like children, making up games as they went: a head popped off a crushed corpse made a fine ball to kick; a pair of disembodied arms became improvised, floppy swords. Darla had chased him through the remains of a church, shrieking with delight as she held the skirts of her dress with one hand and tried to spank him with the severed limb of a nun.

And then they'd heard it, from beneath them. A faint cry for help.

"What have we here?" Angelus said. "Buried treasure, mayhaps?"

Darla giggled. "Do you think they'd want to play with us?"

"'Oh, I'm sure of it," Angelus replied with a grin. "They're already playing hide-and-seek, now, aren't they?"

He took off his black frock coat and began clearing debris, throwing aside chunks of rubble and oaken beams it would take three normal men to move. In no time at all he had a section of floor-boards exposed.

He knelt and put his mouth close to the floor. "Compose yourselves!" he called down. "I've got a team of five men working like mad!" Darla laughed out loud, and he shushed her with a grin on his face.

"Please," came the faint reply. A woman's voice. ". . . we've been trapped down here for five days, with no food or water . . ."

"How many are you?"

". . .three . . ."

"And how'd you get down there, anyway?"

". . . there's a trap-door, in the west corner . . . it leads to the cellar . . ."

"What? All this work, and you mean we've been doing it in the wrong place? Well, I suppose we'll just have start all over—after lunch, of course."

". . . what?"

"Yes, a nice big meal of roast chicken and fresh baked bread and some nice cold water to wash it down—just the thing, don't you think?"

". . . yes, please, just hurry . . ."

"Oh, we won't be long," Angelus said with a chuckle. "An hour or two at the *most.*"

Angelus stood up and dusted off his hands. "All that talking about food has me famished. Shall we go sample the local cuisine?"

"What, you're giving up now? All that work and no reward?"

"Oh, they'll keep," Angelus said cheerfully. "It's like having a fully stocked larder now, isn't it? We can come back and have a nibble whenever we want . . ."

The right-hand branch of the tunnel had angled upward again, though Angel wasn't sure how close he was to the surface. He wondered if maybe he'd chosen the wrong path to follow.

The attack came without warning.

The Quake demon had molded itself into the dirt of the tunnel wall, where it was almost invisible—until one of its fists lashed out and connected with Angel's face.

He dropped the Mag-lite and staggered back as the demon pulled itself out of the wall. The creature's skin was armored in rock that looked like chunks of black glass, sharp-edged crags jutting from every inch of its short, muscular body. Black stalactites hung from its heavy brow and jaw like oily icicles, and when it opened its mouth to snarl at him, Angel saw the same black spikes within.

"Should have brought a pickax," Angel muttered as he reached into his trenchcoat. "Guess this'll have to do . . ."

He drew the double-bladed battle-ax from its special sheath in one smooth motion, swinging it one-handed as the Quake demon lunged forward. He caught the thing across the chest, raising a flash of sparks as steel screeched against stone.

It grabbed for him with a massive hand sporting black claws bigger than a grizzly's. He evaded its clutch, got a two-handed grip on the ax and swung at the thing's skull.

It bounced off, the impact nearly jarring the weapon from Angel's hands. It also knocked the demon back a step—but that was about it.

"Right," Angel said. "No problem."

It rushed at him again. He turned its own momentum against it, dropping his ax at the last second and hip-tossing it to the ground. It was like flipping a Buick; Angel thought he'd come close to breaking his own leg with the maneuver.

But it was facedown in the dirt in front of him— and an instant later, Angel had his ax back in hand.

He chopped down with all his strength, nailing it right between the shoulder blades as it began to get up. The impact drove it down again, but didn't seem to do any other damage.

He hit it again.

And again.

And again.

It kept rising, slowly. On the fifth blow, he broke the head off the ax. All he'd done was to chip a few shards from his opponent's armor.

He leapt on the demon's back as it made it to its feet. Maybe he could break the thing's neck. He seized its head in both hands and wrenched it to the side as hard as he could. It was like trying to turn the steering wheel on a bus encased in cement.

Something whacked Angel in the back of the head hard enough to make his vision blur. He stubbornly kept his grip on the demon's head.

The next blow caught him on the shoulder, making his left arm go numb. He spun to face his new attacker—at first, he thought it was a giant snake.

It wasn't. Somehow, he had failed to notice the Quake demon had a tail.

It was about six feet long, as thick around as a telephone pole. Its tip looked very much like the business end of an oversized garden spade, if garden spades were made out of glossy black rock and doubled as killing weapons.

The tail swung at Angel again, knocking him to his knees. A rocky claw locked around his left wrist. Another gripped his right shoulder.

A shockwave rippled between the two points, slamming up his arm and across his chest. It felt like grabbing a high-voltage line while having a heart attack—though that was just an educated guess on Angel's part, his two-hundred-and-forty-odd years of existence being woefully deficient in both electric and cardiac phenomena.

And it got worse. He could feel his bones begin to hum as his muscles convulsed. In another moment his teeth would explode like firecrackers. . . .

His right arm was still free. He reached up and grabbed the demon's wrist, wrenching its claw loose from its grip on Angel's shoulder. Now he had it by one wrist and it had him by the other.

Angel put every ounce of his strength into a lunge to the side. He took the Quake demon with him—and both its rocky paws plunged into the soft earth of the tunnel.

Angel's body stopped shaking itself apart, and the ground began to shudder instead. Something Angel had learned over the years was that it was generally a lot harder to turn off a mystic source of energy than it was to turn it on . . . and whatever force the demon was generating probably had a much greater affinity for rock and earth than undead flesh.

He was still congratulating himself on his ingenuity when the tunnel collapsed.

CHAPTER TWO

"Buried alive," Darla said. "My, my. How perfectly awful."

"Oh, I don't know," Angelus said. "You know what they say: first you die, then you're buried, then the worms come and eat your flesh. Be grateful for the order in which it occurs."

They had returned from their foray through the remains of Lisbon, after dining on a gang of looters that had the bad judgment to try and rob them. Darla had enjoyed the meal, but Angelus had found them a little greasy for his taste.

And now . . . now they were in the mood for some entertainment.

Angelus picked up a length of wood and strode over to the spot he'd cleared of rubble. He rapped sharply on the floor with it.

"Hello, down there! Still among the living?"

". . . yes! Yes, please, get us out . . ."

"Patience, my friends, patience. It's hard work, slaving under this broiling sun." Angelus smiled broadly at his own joke. "We'll have that trapdoor cleared any minute now. In the meantime, why don't you tell us a bit about yourselves?"

". . . I–I don't know what you mean, sir . . ."

"Well, are we rescuing whores or nuns? The right answer will have my men digging faster, I can tell you that."

Darla had to cover her mouth to suppress her laughter.

". . . neither, sir. We're parishioners, who were in the church when the earth began to shake. The priest thought we would be safe here . . ."

"And where is the good Father?"

". . . he . . . he wasn't quick enough, when the roof began to fall . . ."

"But *you* were, weren't you? Bolted like a rabbit for a hole, I'd imagine; didn't put an elbow in the dear Father's chest in your hurry, did you?"

"No! No, I swear . . ."

"What's your name, my dear?"

"Maria . . ."

"And your two friends? Why haven't I heard from them?"

"Francesco is hurt, he does not move or speak.

25

Estrellita is trapped in the far corner under a fallen timber . . ."

"And you? Are you injured?"

". . . I think my arm is broken . . ."

"Well, look on the bright side—you've still got the other one, haven't you?" Angelus toyed idly with the piece of wood he held. "Do you think you can do me a favor?"

". . . I'll do whatever I can . . ."

"Sing."

". . . what?"

"Sing us a song, to help the lads work. To get them movin', like."

". . . my throat is so dry . . ."

"The louder you sing, the quicker you'll get some water. That's fair now, isn't it?"

". . . what . . . what should I . . ."

"D'ye have any favorites, my sweet?" Angelus asked Darla with a grin.

" 'Ave Maria,' perhaps?" Darla suggested.

"That's no song to work by!" Angelus declared. "Say, d'ye know any good Irish drinking songs?"

". . . please, I'm so thirsty . . ."

"Perhaps a hymn is appropriate, after all. What about 'The Old Hundredth'? Always a favorite in our church—though I have to admit, my attendance was hardly perfect. *For why? The Lord our God is good, His mercy is forever sure,*" Angelus sang. *"His*

26

truth at all times firmly stood, and shall from age to age endure! Come on, now, raise your voice in praise!"

". . . Praise, praise God, from whom all blessings flow . . ."

"Louder!"

"Praise him all creatures here below . . ."

Angelus extended an arm toward Darla. "Would you care to dance, m'lady?"

She came to him. They laughed together as the faint, quavering voice drifted up from the ground beneath their feet.

"Praise him above, ye heavenly host . . ."

The memory of that voice echoed through Angel's skull as his consciousness slowly returned. He could almost smell Lisbon, burning still. . . .

Except his nose was full of dirt.

Since breathing was more or less optional for vampires, that wasn't a problem. However, the fact that he was now buried alive—well, buried undead, actually—was. At least he was alone; the Quake demon was gone, or at least no longer had Angel in a vibrating death-grip. The dirt around him wasn't that tightly packed, either; he must be close to the surface.

As Angel started to claw his way upward, he couldn't help thinking about Darla. The first time he'd done this was after she'd bitten him—but then it was his own grave he was digging his way out of.

He remembered the panic of waking in his own coffin, of thinking there'd been some terrible mistake, of pushing up on the lid and feeling the heavy weight of wet earth holding it down. He'd pounded on the lid until it smashed under his new strength, and then he'd frantically, blindly clawed his way upward. Even though his body no longer needed air, his brain hadn't figured that out yet; his lungs burned with a desire they no longer had, a need they merely imagined.

Angel had never known the difference between want and need back then. If he wanted something, he took it; if he needed to brawl or drink or womanize, he did it. It was all the same, and when he'd become a vampire, he'd continued in much the same way. His needs changed, but his attitude toward them did not.

And then he'd regained his soul, and everything was different.

Suddenly, all he wanted was relief from the immense burden of guilt that descended upon him, and when he realized no relief was possible, he had wanted to suffer. No—he'd *needed* to. He'd needed to atone for all the mayhem, all the corpses strewn in his wake, and for a hundred years he'd done exactly that. He'd lived as little more than an animal, drinking the blood of vermin and sleeping in sewers. It had taken him a century to find the desire to do anything other than exist.

There was a very clear line between what Angel wanted and what he needed, now. What he wanted, deep down, was what everyone wanted: to be happy. But if Angel were ever to experience even a single moment of true happiness, the Gypsy curse placed on him would rip the soul out of his body, transforming him once more into the monster known as Angelus. Angel could never have what he wanted.

But he could have what he needed—because all he needed was to fight back the darkness that he used to live in. To make the shadows of the world a little safer.

Twenty minutes later, Angel's head popped out of the middle of a baseball field. The sky was the rosy color of predawn, droplets of dew glinting on the green crewcut of the grass. Angel pulled himself out of the earth just behind first base, then took out his cell phone—luckily it hadn't been crushed. He made a quick call as he headed for the nearest manhole.

All the way back to the office, he couldn't get that hymn out of his head.

"Demon Urban Professionals? We're working for *Duppies?*" Cordelia said, putting her issue of *Vogue* down on her desk. "Great. How do you kill one—drive an Ikea catalog through its heart?"

"Expose its stock portfolio t'direct sunlight," Doyle offered from where he sprawled on the office couch. "Might even have to carry a hood ornament from a Mercedes, instead of a cross."

"Very funny," Angel said. "But—demons or not—they have a real problem."

"Big deal," Cordelia snorted. "They're *demons*, right? Just because they can afford pedicures for their little hooved feet doesn't mean we're suddenly best buds. I say, let them eat dirt."

"A major earthquake could have all of California eating dirt," Angel pointed out. "Including you."

"Oh," Cordelia said. "Good point. Plus, having Hollywood destroyed would *not* be good for my career."

"And it doesn't sound like they've got hooved feet, either," Doyle said. "Actually, they sound pretty normal. For demons, I mean." He glanced over at Cordelia.

"*Normal?* What about that tongue-flicky-thingy? Please."

. . . *please* . . .

"—isn't that right, Angel?" Doyle asked.

"What? I, uh, wasn't paying attention."

"I said, y'can't judge a book by its cover. Or a demon by its tongue, for that matter. And speakin'

30

of tongues, Angel, what were you planning t'say if you got caught wanderin' around down there without a hall pass?"

"Actually," Angel said, "I came up with this really clever cover story. I was going to tell them—"

"That's ridiculous," Cordelia said. "I mean, if the cover of a book doesn't matter, then why are there so many different kinds? What do they pay cover artists and graphic designers and photographers for? If covers *really* weren't important, books would all look the same and people would think Fabio was a brand of stain remover."

"Uh, right," Angel said. "The thing is, I'd like to know a little more about both races. If we're going to jump into the middle of a war, I want to make sure we're on the right side."

"I vote for the side *without* demons on it," Cordelia said.

"Does that include vampires?" a rich tenor asked from the doorway. "Or just vampires with souls?"

Galvin strolled through the door. He wore a dark blue silk suit and a wide smile.

"And you are?" Cordelia asked.

"This is our client," Angel said. "Galvin, these are my associates, Cordelia and Doyle."

"Doyle! A fine Irish name," Galvin said, shaking Doyle's hand. "Meaning the dark stranger, or the new arrival. Perhaps that's more appropriate for me, eh?"

He turned to Cordelia. "And Cordelia, another Celt if I'm not mistaken. 'The sea's jewel.'"

Cordelia frowned. "Seize my what?"

"Well, with a fine group of fellow countrymen like this working for you, you have my full confidence, Angel. Allow me to express myself in monetary terms." Galvin pulled out a checkbook.

"That's all right—" Angel started.

"—perfectly all right, we accept checks no problem," Cordelia finished. "And being paid at the beginning instead of the end is actually our policy, because we can do a *much* better job if we can just pay for things instead of worrying about receipts and stuff."

"Of course," Galvin said. He filled in the check, ripped it out of the book and handed it to Cordelia. "I hope this is sufficient for a retainer."

Cordelia glanced at it. "That'll be fine," she said. She opened the top drawer of her desk and put the check inside, closed the drawer, clasped her hands together in front of her and smiled up at Galvin. "Now—what can we do for you?"

"Angel already told me what happened when he called," Galvin said. "I just wanted to come down and have a look around myself. And offer an invitation, in person."

"That's not neccesary," Angel said. "I only need to be invited to a place once to be able to enter—"

"No, no, no," Galvin said with a chuckle. "I meant a proper invitation—to a party. Appletree Estates is having a little get-together tonight, and we'd like you to come. If you're going to be looking out for our welfare, we'd like to get to know you a bit."

"That's very kind, Galvin, but—"

"—we couldn't go unless you let us bring something," Doyle interrupted.

"Well, we always appreciate a good bottle of wine," Galvin said. "And we never turn away a body with whiskey, either."

"We'll see you tonight, then," Doyle said.

"Excellent." Galvin stifled a yawn. "Excuse me. I really must be getting home; I can barely keep my eyes open during the day. Fortunately, my limo has a human driver—I'm sure I'd doze off at the wheel. I'll see you all tonight." He nodded good-bye and left.

"Well, that was—" Angel started, then stopped.

"What?" Doyle asked.

"I was just waiting for one of you to finish my sentence," Angel said. "Since you both seem to be so good at it."

"*EEEEEEE!*" Cordelia shrieked.

Doyle jumped to his feet and Angel whirled around, tensing for trouble.

Cordelia had the check in both hands.

"Did you see how much this is *for? Oh my God!*"

"Bit of a delayed reaction, Cordy?" Doyle asked.

"No. I just *internalized* it until he left. I *am* an actress, you know."

"I'm not sure it's a good idea to socialize with clients," Angel said.

"Don't think of it as socializin'," Doyle said, settling back onto the couch. "Think of it as research. You said yourself we need to know more about these Serpentene guys. This is the perfect opportunity to feel 'em out."

"I was thinking more along the lines of spending a few hours doing some reading—"

"Oh, no," Cordelia said. "Reading or fighting, those are your solutions to everything. You're like the Bruce Lee of bookworms. You should get out and enjoy yourself a little more—and this check is *definitely* a reason to celebrate."

"I'd rather do my research over a pint than a page," Doyle said. "What do you say? Between the three of us, I'm sure we can—"

"Um, excuse me?" Cordelia said. "I hope by 'the three of us' you mean you, Angel and an imaginary friend, because no *way* am I partying in a basement full of walking boa constrictors. I mean, sure, I'll take their money—but what if there's another quake and we get trapped down there? They'll turn me into Cordelia-jerky faster than a marooned soccer team."

"That's also a consideration," Angel admitted. "I don't want to put either of you in danger."

"Look, man," Doyle said reasonably. "It boils down t'this: *somebody's* got t'go, to check these guys out. You're the one they hired, so you gotta make an appearance. Now, if you go alone, you know you're just gonna do your lurking-in-the-corner-lookin'-uncomfortable thing, and you won't find out bugger-all. Me, though, I know how t'work a room; gimme a couple drinks and a little mood music, I'll have the clan history on the back of a cocktail napkin in half an hour."

"Okay, so you and I go—"

"—and I'm not goin' unless Cordy does."

"What?" Cordelia snapped.

"Come on, Cordy, it'll be fun. And with you there, we'll learn twice as much. Who could say no to those big, beautiful eyes?"

"Well . . ."

"Then it's settled," Doyle said. "Tonight, we *mingle!*"

"I'll see you guys later, then," Cordelia said, getting up and grabbing her coat.

"Where are you going?" Angel asked.

"To get ready, of course."

"Cordelia, it's two in the afternoon."

"Look, if I have to go to this—this demonfest, I will. But demons or not, they obviously have money and they know how to dress. Unless you want them to treat me like the drive-thru girl at Burger World, you better let me do some preparation. That means new hair, shoes and wardrobe, all on the microscopic salary you pay me. I need the rest of the day, minimum, to put together a look that doesn't scream Salvation Army."

"'Uh—okay . . .'"

When Cordelia had left, Angel said, "You didn't have to force her to come along."

"Oh, come on, man," Doyle said, getting up from the couch. "You know as well as I do that not all demons are bad news—but Cordy's a little unclear on the concept. If I can't get her to see some demons as at least being on our side, what chance is there that she'd consider dating one?"

"You're only half-demon, Doyle."

"Like that's gonna make a difference. 'Hey, Cordy, only one side of my family hails from the Infernal Pit, but maybe Thanksgiving with *your* folks is a better idea.' She'd love that."

"Doyle, you haven't even asked her out yet and you're already planning where to spend the holidays."

"Yeah, well, it's never too soon to start planning a dysfunctional relationship." Doyle jammed his hands into his pockets and frowned. "Thanks for goin' along with this, though. It's about as close as I can see to me and Cordy going on a date."

"You're going to have to tell her eventually."

"I know, I know. Just give me some time . . ."

A young, blond Serpentene woman in a short black dress met them at the front door of the complex. "Hi," she said. "I'm Kyra. Come with me."

She ushered them through the lobby and into the elevator. Once the doors had closed, she pulled out a key and inserted it into the elevator's control panel. "This is how we stay hidden," she informed them. "We rent out the upper floors to humans, but we're careful to never ride with them."

The doors opened on the first Serpentene floor. "Galvin's the one throwing the party," Kyra said, leading them down the hall. "Wait 'til you see his place—it's *amazing.*"

"Aren't you worried the upstairs tenants might hear the . . . festivities?" Angel asked.

"There's studio-quality soundproofing between our floors and the rest of the building," Kyra answered. "We don't have to worry about noise."

Cordelia shot Angel a look. He knew exactly what she was thinking: *and it conveniently muffles all sorts of ruckus, like the horrible screams when we murder our party guests.*

Galvin met them at the door. "Angel, Doyle, Cordelia! I'm so glad you made it!" He beamed at them happily. "Come in, come in—let me show you around."

The suite was large, at least seven rooms, and full of people. Galvin took obvious pride in showing off his acquisitions: the living room boasted a Picasso, a Rembrandt and a Van Gogh; the master bedroom contained a Louis XIV bed; the library had first editions from Dickens, Poe and Twain. Even the bathroom held a Ming Dynasty vase.

When the tour was over, Galvin apologized for being a poor host. "Here I am blathering over all my worldly goods, and you don't even have a drink in hand to dull the pain! Come, let's do something about that."

He led them over to the bar, a massive chunk of teak that took up most of one wall. "What's your pleasure? We have a fine selection of single malts, both scotch and whiskey. Or perhaps you'd prefer wine, or beer? We have Guinness on tap, and an excellent oatmeal stout."

"Uh, we brought this," Doyle said. He held out a bottle-shaped paper bag.

Galvin took it, opened it, peered inside. "Ah," he said. "How nice. We'll just put that here for later, shall we?"

Doyle looked around the room as Galvin poured drinks. Everyone seemed young, attractive and well-dressed. *If this wasn't L.A.*, Doyle thought, *it'd almost be creepy.*

Maureen, the Serpentene woman Angel had met yesterday, came up to them. She wore an evening gown of pale yellow and emeralds at her throat and ears. "Hello again," she said.

Angel introduced Doyle and Cordelia, and they nodded hello. Galvin excused himself as more guests arrived, leaving the four of them alone.

There was a moment's awkward silence.

"So—you're a demon," Cordelia said brightly. "What's *that* like?"

"What she means is—" Doyle interjected hastily, "she's never—uh, she's not experienced with—"

Maureen laughed. "It's all right. We spend so much time hiding, it's refreshing to encounter honesty for a change." She took a sip from her glass of white wine. "Actually, if I'm going to be honest—and remember, you started it—it's a little scary, too."

"I can understand that," Doyle said. "Bein' afraid of what people might think if they knew the real you, and all. Well, don't worry; we're here for a good time, not an interrogation."

"Actually, there *are* a few things I need to ask Galvin," Angel said. "If you'll excuse me?" He slipped away.

"Good ol' Angel—always on the job," Doyle said. "If that boy were wound any tighter he could run a clock."

"We're used to it," Maureen said. "That kind of attitude, I mean. We're all sort of workaholics, here."

"What exactly do you work *at*, anyway?" Cordelia asked.

"I'm a sales rep for Neiman-Marcus."

Cordelia's eyes widened. "What department?"

"Women's fashions, mostly."

"And I'll bet you get a big employee's discount, don't you—"

"You know it. You should see the line that just came in—"

The conversation shifted to fashion. Doyle, whose fashion sense Cordelia once described as "thrift store lounge lizard," felt his eyes beginning to glaze over after the first two minutes. He excused himself to go use the bathroom; Maureen and Cordelia hardly noticed he'd left.

"So, Galvin," Angel said. "Are all the Serpentene Irish?"

"Aye, it's where we hail from," Galvin said, affecting a thick brogue for a moment. He picked his drink up from the white grand piano he'd set it down on. "Not for some time, though. Not a one of us has set foot on our native soil since we were banished. Much like you, we can't go where we're not wanted."

"It wouldn't be Saint Patrick who banished you, would it?"

"Well, of course it was! Where d'you think all those snakes went? To America, land of opportunity."

"In the fifth century?"

"So we had a few detours along the way. I understand you've been down a few roads yourself."

"I've . . . done my share of traveling," Angel said.

The smell of the lemon trees mingling with the odor of charred wood and decaying flesh. The cries of the gulls as they fought over the bodies of the dead . . .

"Yes, you were quite . . . notorious, throughout Europe. Or rather, Angelus was."

"That wasn't me," Angel said flatly.

"I realize that," Galvin said gently. "And I apolo gize if I've offended you. I just thought it best if you understood: we know about your past, and we know that it is history, nothing more. That we do not judge you by the horrific reputation of Angelus, but by the honorable standards you have established since you regained your soul. We know we are not the first demons you've helped—but we *would* like to be the most grateful."

"That's . . . very kind," Angel said, fumbling for words. "Thank you."

"You're very welcome. The basis of a good friendship is simple, I've always found: you forgive your companions for not being perfect, and they do the same for you."

"We could all use a little forgiveness," Angel said.

"Father, forgive me, for I have sinned," Angelus intoned. "Come on now, I'm sure a good Catholic like you knows the words."

The voice from beneath the floorboards sounded weaker. ". . . f–forgive me, Father . . ."

The voice trailed off. Silence.

"Come on, now," Angelus urged. "How can I give you the last rites if you don't confess your sins first?"

"Tell her you're the Pope," Darla said. "At this point, she'll believe anything."

"Maria?" Angelus asked. "You still there, darlin'?"

". . . why . . . why do I need the last rites? I thought you were going to . . . rescue us . . ."

"Purely a formality, my dear. In case we don't make it in time. You wouldn't want to be spending eternity roasting in Hell over a technicality, would you?"

". . . no . . ."

"Then go ahead. Tell me your sins."

". . . I . . . I had an argument with my mother, the last time I saw her. I was disrespectful when she wanted me to do the washing . . ."

Darla snorted. "A dispute over laundry. Boring. I don't want to hear about the insignificant details of her tiny life—"

"Shhhhh," Angelus said, glaring at her.

". . . and now . . . I don't know . . ."

"You don't know if you'll ever see your poor mother again," Angelus said. "Or if she went to her grave with anger in her heart, anger toward an ungrateful child that wouldn't do something as simple as washing a few clothes. Is that it?"

A choked sobbing was Maria's only reply.

Angelus straightened up and gave Darla a satisfied smile. "It's not the big things, darlin'," he said to her. "It's the insignificant details that worm their way into your soul . . ."

Doyle was lost.

At least, that's what he was going to tell any of the Serpentene if they questioned where he was, which was strolling down the hallway away from the party.

In Doyle's experience, people with a lot of money always had something to hide. Of course, sometimes that thing was just a big heap of money, but not always. More often than not it was something illegal, immoral, or really disgusting. The Serpentene had gone from completely secretive to we-want-to-be-best-friends way too fast for Doyle; he'd been around enough scam artists to recognize the taste of blarney when it was being fed to him.

So it was time for a little look around—without a

guide. Hopefully, he could discover something useful. Why, he might even impress Cordy . . .

"This is impressive," Cordelia said. "What did you say it was called again?"

"Lagavulin," answered Maureen, taking a sip from her own glass of cut crystal. She and Cordelia were standing by the bar while a young Serpentene named Ian poured them drinks. Ian, Cordelia decided, had a kind of Sting-like quality to him, but with better hair. He was wearing a charcoal Armani suit and managed to make it look casual.

"I'm not really much of a hard alcohol kind of person," Cordelia said, "more of a white wine spritzer girl, you know? But this is really yummy—how much did you say it costs?"

"Around two hundred a bottle. But it's not the best Galvin stocks, not by a mile. Try some of *this*." Ian poured another shot into her glass. "It's called Glenfarcus, and it's older than you are."

Cordelia took a sip. "Wow. It's so *smooth* . . . is that the right term, or do you have your own scotchy language like wine drinkers? It goes down real easy, anyway."

"Aye," Ian said with a grin. "Aye, that it does . . ."

Doyle had been up and down three hallways before he found it, in a room marked STORAGE, just off the telemarketing center. The door wasn't locked.

The room was lined with shelves. At first glance, Doyle was reminded of a police evidence room; everything was bagged and tagged.

But he wasn't looking at rows of impounded weapons and drugs. The items on the shelves varied so widely he wasn't sure what they had in common: they ranged from toys to canisters of film. He picked up a teddy bear in a clear plastic bag and looked at the tag. "S. Powell, 12/25/57," he whispered to himself. "Kinda late for a Christmas present . . ."

Other items were marked the same way, just a name and a date. He examined an old pair of jeans, a framed photo of someone's grandmother, a cookbook—he couldn't figure out the connection between them.

And then he heard footsteps.

"Gluck?" Galvin asked.

"Gluck is good," Angel answered after a moment's consideration. "Especially *Armide*. Although Haydn's *Symphony Number 22 in E-Flat* is still one of my favorites."

Galvin was seated at the piano now, and he tinkled out a few notes. "I was there when Haydn was appointed Kapellmeister to Prince Esterhazy, in 1761," Galvin said. "Quite the affair."

"You're older than you look."

"But not quite as well-preserved as you," Galvin said with a chuckle. "Long life—another thing we have in common. But unlike vampires, we do age; we just shed our skins every few years, which keeps us looking young. I've let this skin get a little wrinkled on purpose—a patriarch should look the part, don't you think?"

"How old—or young—you look does matter," Angel admitted. "I saw Mozart on his first European tour. He was six years old. Sixteen years later, when Beethoven went on *his* first tour, they claimed *he* was six—actually, he was eight." Angel shook his head. "People always lie about their age in show business . . ."

The footsteps receded. "Time t'go," Doyle muttered to himself. He waited another minute, then slipped out the door.

Back at the party, no one even seemed to notice he'd been gone; Doyle wasn't sure if he should feel relieved or insulted. One feeling was becoming more and more clear, though.

Doyle didn't belong.

It wasn't something coming from the Serpentene; they all smiled and responded pleasantly whenever he tried to join a conversation. Problem was, Doyle couldn't relate to anything they were saying. He didn't know much about the stock market or antique furniture or vintage wines, and after his fifth failed attempt to start a discussion on the merits of the Dodgers versus the Padres, he gave up.

Doyle had never felt like he fitted in, even before he'd learned about his half-demon heritage. People seemed to sense there was something strange about him; it made him work all the harder to be likable. Be quick enough with a drink or a joke, and they won't have time to reject you, Doyle told himself . . . but still, nobody seemed to hang around very long. He had many acquaintances but few friends. Sometimes, he thought that's all he really wanted—a true friend. Somebody who accepted him for himself, somebody who wasn't a demon or a vampire or anything else—just a nice, normal person. Somebody to make him feel like he belonged.

Of course, he thought to himself. *And who do you fancy? Miss Cordelia Chase, who wouldn't touch a demon with a ten-foot pole-ax and a note from her mother. Ah, Doyle, you must be outta your mind.*

He joined Cordelia at the bar. And despite Cordelia's often-stated aversion to creatures demonic, she *did* seem to be enjoying herself. . . .

"You know, I can't decide which one is my favorite," Cordelia said. "Now *this* one I like. I really, really *do.*" She lifted her glass and drained it.

47

"Mmmm. It tastes like dirt, but in a *good* way. A good way, y'know?"

"That's the peat," Maureen said.

"Well, old Pete *definitely* knows his Scotch, that's all I have to say . . . but that one's good, too. And that one. And that one. And that one, too."

"Uh, Cordy?" Doyle said. "How many have you had?"

"Just a *few*," Cordelia said. "To be soshabubble. Excuse me."

"I think she's had enough," Doyle said. "Stay here—I'm gonna get Angel."

"And where would I go?" Cordelia said with an exaggerated shrug. "I'm happy right *here*. Even if here *is* five stories underground with a buncha snakes. N'offense."

"None taken," Ian said with a grin.

"—saw Handel's *Messiah* in London *and* Berlin," Angel was saying to Galvin when Doyle walked up. "And in my opinion—what?"

"Cordy's a little—well, looped," Doyle said. "I think we should take her home."

"All right. Galvin, it looks like we'll have to be leaving. Thank you for your hospitality, though."

"Our pleasure," Galvin said. "It's been a while since I had this enjoyable a discussion about music."

Back at the bar, Cordelia was telling Maureen, "I hope you didn't take that remark about dirt the wrong way. I understand that dirt is very *important* to you people. Well, it is to me, *too*. Without dirt there would be nothing for things to be on *top* of. Except other things. And then everything would have to be *balanced*. And you know what? That's not as easy as it *looks*." She fell out of her chair.

Angel and Doyle caught her before she hit the carpet. "Good night, ladies," Doyle said, shaking his head. "Could we get someone with an elevator key to let us out?"

On the drive home, Doyle rode with Cordelia in the back of Angel's convertible. "*Please* don't let her throw up on the upholstery," Angel told him. "If there's one thing I don't miss about being human, it's the smell of recycled food."

"Oh, m'fine," Cordelia said. "Can we stop at a Wendy's? I want one of those square hamburgers. Hey, howcum they don't have square buns, huh? I mean, haven't they heard of *bread?* And robots."

"What?" Doyle said.

"Robots. *They* have square buns." She started giggling.

"Geez, Cordy, you're really loaded," Doyle said. "I mean, I been on a few benders in my time, and on the hungry-drunk and non sequitur scale, you're somewhere between a lost weekend and Spring Break."

The car slipped through the California night. Oncoming headlights threw shadows across the interior that moved like living things. Doyle could smell the petrochemical tang of asphalt cooling after a hot day, mixed in with a breeze from the ocean. Summer midnight in L.A.

"I'm cold," Cordelia said. She snuggled up to Doyle; after a second's hesitation he put his arm around her.

"Y'want me to tell Angel to put the top up?"

"No. This is good." She looked up into his face. "Y'know, you are actually very cute. Inna Irish way. Did you know that?"

"I've heard rumors."

She laughed. "And you're *funny*. I *like* you, Doyle. Inna Irish way."

"I think right now it's more a *Scotch* way, Cordy. But thanks just the same."

A gentle snore came from beside him.

Doyle sighed.

CHAPTER THREE

Darla and Angelus returned to the barge to sleep away the daylight hours, but not before they'd taken a few precautions; they moved the barge from the river to the bay, anchoring offshore to reduce the risk of uninvited visitors. They could still be boarded, but the looters seemed to be concentrating their attention on the smoldering corpse of the city.

Before that, though, they had to take care of their "buried treasure."

"Maria!" Angelus called down. "I've got some bad news, darlin' . . ."

". . . what's wrong? Oh God, you can't get us out, can you?"

"Now, now, dear, nothing like that. It's just that the Spaniards are comin'."

". . . I don't understand . . ."

"Spain is taking advantage of the disaster; they're tryin' t'take the whole country. It's said they're slaughtering all the survivors they come across. We have to take cover until tomorrow, for fear of bein' discovered. You wouldn't want that, would you?"

". . . no . . ."

"Good. We'll be back under cover of darkness, but you have to stay quiet until we return. No callin' for help—"

"No. No! You can't leave us here! Francesco is dead and maybe Estrellita too and we'll *die*, don't you understand? *You can't leave us here!*"

"Well, well," Darla said with a smirk. "Looks like you pushed her just a little too far. A pity; hysterics are only entertaining for the first minute or so."

"I'm not done yet," Angelus shot back. "Maria! Maria! Calm down, darlin'."

". . . you can't, you can't . . ."

"Shhhhh! Listen. Listen and tell me what you hear."

". . . what? I hear . . . gnawing. It sounds like rats, chewing on wood . . ."

"Not rats, darlin'. It's a drill. I'll be through these floorboards in a minute. There. Can you see the hole?"

"Yes! Yes, I see it!"

"Get your mouth underneath it. I'm going to pour some water down . . ." Angelus upended a canteen and watched the cool, clear water gurgle into the hole he'd made. He listened carefully; when he heard Maria's frantic, choked gulping, he smiled.

"That's right, drink deep. We wouldn't want you perishin' of thirst while we're away . . ."

"Mornin', Cordy," Doyle said.

Cordelia managed to glare at him through a pair of sunglasses as she entered the office and took off her coat. "Don't talk to me. Don't even *think* at me until I've had coffee."

"You . . . sound a little upset." Doyle rubbed the back of his head and looked uncomfortable.

"Upset? I spent the first twenty minutes of my day reviewing what I ate over the last twelve hours. Reviewing in a very unpleasant way that I would prefer not to discuss, so just shut up, okay?"

"Bit of a rough night, I guess."

"I wouldn't know. The last thing I remember is drinking with someone named Pete. Or maybe Glen. Did we go to Wendy's?"

"It was suggested," Doyle said. "But cooler heads prevailed."

"Huh. Anyway, the next thing I know I wake up in my own bed, which is doing a pretty good impression of a Tilt-a-Whirl. Doyle, you have to tell me—did I do anything . . ."

"Anything what?"

"You know. Embarrassing."

"Well, the striptease on top of the bar was a bit much, but I think y'redeemed yourself when you wouldn't go past your underwear. It's that kind of restraint that shows real class."

"Doyle, I'm warning you—"

Doyle sighed, then shook his head and smiled. "Cordy, you didn't do anything . . . wrong. Nothin' you should be ashamed of. I swear."

She squinted at him suspiciously. "Well . . . okay."

Angel walked in from his office. He looked up from the open book in his hands. "Morning, Cordelia. How's your head?"

"My head is fine. It's not currently firmly attached and is having a nasty little war with the rest of my body, but I can handle it. Just don't ask me to do anything loud, like work."

"Up to doing some research? Or would the crash of turning pages be too much?"

"You mean reading about demons? Descriptions of the horrible things they've done, the horrible things they plan on doing and the horrible things they do in their spare time? Boy oh boy, my stomach can hardly wait. Maybe I should just go throw up now."

"I was thinking more along the lines of checking the Serpentene's credentials in the business community—"

"No, I really meant the throwing up part. Excuse me." Cordelia hurried out of the room.

Angel stared after her for a second, then shrugged and went back to leafing through his book.

Doyle walked up to him. "I still can't believe it."

"Get over it, Doyle," Angel said without looking up.

"But it's never *happened* to me before."

"It happens."

"Has it ever happened to you?"

Angel looked up, considered it for a moment. "Having a girl pass out on my shoulder? Not . . . exactly."

"Yeah, well, havin' someone shuffle off to dreamland while you're drainin' the life out of 'em isn't the same thing, is it?"

"Look, Doyle, she had a lot to drink; it doesn't have anything to do with your . . . *manhood*. If anything, you should take it as a compliment."

"How d'you figure?"

"She obviously trusted you enough to let go."

Doyle thought for a moment, then nodded. "I guess that's one way of lookin' at it."

"And remember—she didn't vomit on you."

"There *is* that . . ."

Cordelia returned from the bathroom. "There—fresh as a daisy. Anybody got a breath mint?"

Angel and Doyle hit the books, while Cordelia made some calls. By midafternoon they knew a little bit more about what they were dealing with.

Quake demons were also known as Tremblors. They were subterranean dwellers who rarely made an appearance on the surface; the only exception seemed to be when collecting victims for a ritual called the Crushing of Souls. The last time such a ritual was said to be performed was in Japan in 1920, causing a devastating earthquake in Tokyo and Yokohama that killed a hundred and twenty thousand people.

The timing of the ritual was based on something called the Dance of the Sleeping Giants; unfortunately, the Tremblors seemed to be the only ones that understood what that meant. The ritual itself required four very specific victims: someone close to air, someone close to water, someone close to fire and someone close to earth.

"Someone close to earth—that would explain why they tried to kidnap one of the Serpentene," Angel said. "But not why they'd want to destroy their home."

"Maybe they're not after the Serpentene specifically," Cordelia said. "Could be they're just in the wrong place at the wrong time. Earthquakes are pretty nondiscriminating."

"True enough," Angel admitted. "But I think there's more to it than that."

"I'd say you were right," Doyle said. "Considering what I found last night."

"You found something?" Cordelia asked.

"Sorry, Cordy," Doyle said. "I forgot your memory is a bit spotty about the evenin's festivities."

"He found a room full of catalogued objects," Angel said.

"What kind of objects? Monkey's paws, heads in jars, that kind of thing?"

"That's the strange part," Doyle said. "They were really ordinary things. Kid's toys, old blue jeans, photo albums. Nothin' ominous about them, except the fact that they were so carefully arranged and labeled."

"Maybe the Serpentene are just really anal," Cordelia said. "I dated a guy like that once. He sewed little labels inside his socks."

"Or maybe the objects are cursed," Doyle said.

"Right," Cordelia said. "Don't put on those pants— they're the *cursed* pants! You'll look fat—*forever*! Puh-*leeze*, Doyle—that's the kind of idea a TV executive would come up with."

"What about voodoo?" Angel suggested. "Snakes figure big in tropical mythologies. Maybe they're using the items for sympathetic magic."

"They want people to feel sorry for them?" Cordelia asked.

"No," Angel said patiently. "Sympathetic magic is when you use an object connected to a person— usually something they've owned, or a photo of them—in a mystic ritual. Whatever you do to the item has the same effect on the person."

"Or maybe they just have a hard time throwing anything away," Cordelia said. "For what it's worth, I didn't get a creepy evil vibe from them at all; I had a really good time. The part I remember, I mean."

"I don't know," Doyle said. "That's not the impression I got. I felt like somethin' was wrong."

"Doyle, you just felt out of place," Cordelia said. "Just because these people appreciate the finer things in life—and by that I do *not* mean cheap beer and pay-per-view wrestling—it doesn't necessarily follow that they're evil."

"Well now," Doyle said. "You sure went from 'forked-tongues-give-me-the-willies' to 'Rah! Rah! Go Snakes!' pretty quick. Maybe Angel should take them up on their offer, too."

"What offer?" Cordelia asked.

"It's nothing," Angel muttered.

"Oh, that's right," Doyle said. "You'd already slipped into a coma by the time Angel mentioned it. Seems that Galvin wants Angel around full-time;

offered him an apartment if he'd take a job with them as a security guard."

"Security *consultant,*" Angel said. "And it wouldn't be full-time; I'd still work here . . . I'd just live there."

"So you're actually *considering* this?" Cordelia asked.

"I didn't say that. I'm just telling you what the offer was—"

"I think you should take it," Cordelia said.

"—what?"

"Seriously," Cordelia said. "Think about it. I mean, after all, they *are* your kind."

"Just because they're demons doesn't mean—"

"I meant young and good-looking," Cordelia said. "Who knows, they might even convince you there are other colors besides black."

"He can't just move in with a client in the middle of a case," Doyle protested.

"Look," Cordelia said. "There is nothing worse than being an outsider. You have no idea how difficult it was for me in high school—it was almost impossible to *avoid* losers like that."

"You think I need a group to belong to?" Angel asked.

"Well, *duh*—it's not like there's a vampire-with-a-soul-private-detective Web site."

"Actually, there's a few," Doyle said.

"Anyway," Cordelia continued, "this is probably as close as you're ever going to get to having drinking buddies—and rich friends are the *best* friends."

"Well, it *was* nice having a conversation that didn't end with one of us crumbling into a pile of dust," Angel admitted. "But Doyle's right; it wouldn't be appropriate for me to involve myself that closely with a client, especially one we don't know the full story on. So—what have you found out?"

"About the Serpentene?" Cordelia said. "Not much. The building is owned by a corporation called Appletree. They own a few other concerns, all of which are members in good standing of the Better Business Bureau. No criminal investigations, no lawsuits, no horrible cult murder-suicides. Pretty clean for a bunch of salesdemons."

"Well, I haven't found out much more, but what I did find out isn't necessarily good," Doyle said. "According to some texts, the snakes the Serpentene are descended from is *the* snake—the one that tempted Adam and Eve."

"Half the demons in the San Fernando Valley make that claim," Angel said. "It's like saying your ancestors came across on the *Mayflower.*"

"Well, it's all I got so far," Doyle said. "But I do have a line on a potential gold mine of information.

Guy by the name of Graedeker, trades in a lot of occult merchandise. If it has t'do with buying, selling, and black magic, he's the one t'talk to."

"Okay, you follow up on that. Now, getting back to the Quake demons—any possible weaknesses?"

"Well," Doyle said, "I found this: 'Only that which opposes it can oppose it.' It's definitely talkin' about the Tremblors, but damned if I know what it means."

"Sounds like it doesn't mean anything," Cordelia said. "It's like saying, 'that which you eat is eaten,' or 'that which you bought on sale was marked down.' "

"We'll keep it in mind," Angel said. "Now, if they need four victims, they may already have some or all of the others. I'll check with Kate on missing persons who might fit the bill."

"And I'll do some more up close and personal research on the Serpentene," Cordelia said. "Maureen and I made a date to go shopping—she's going to buy me a new outfit! See you guys later . . ."

"First things first," Angelus said. "Let's go check on our little trapped rat." He got out of bed and began pulling on clothes.

Darla frowned at him from where she reclined, nude. "I think I'm getting jealous. You actually care more about your little Maria than *this*?" She ran one hand down a perfect, creamy-white thigh.

"Not that it's not temptin', darlin'," Angelus said, flashing her a smile. "But I think you and I both know where my interests lie."

Darla shook her head and laughed. "Torment over sex. You are a piece of work, my love."

"Some men are fighters, some are lovers. Me, now, I think my true callin' is somethin' else; I was born to be a right bastard."

"Well, you *are* good at it. I've just never seen you draw one out quite this long."

"I know, I know. I think it's because I never had a pet as a child. It's just so enjoyable *playing* with her . . ."

Darla stretched lazily and got out of bed. "So what games will we be playing today?"

"I figure she must be gettin' right hungry by now. Hunger can make you do terrible things—and those other bodies in there with her are just going to waste. . . ."

But when they got to the ruins of the church, they were not the first to arrive.

Four men were busy clearing rubble by lantern-light. They were obviously working to uncover the trapdoor in the west corner.

"Ah, Maria, Maria," Angelus said under his breath. "You bad, ungrateful girl. You've been talkin' to strangers—and after all the warnings I gave you, too."

He and Darla strode forward. One of the men, a dark-skinned Portuguese, looked up as they approached. "You there!" the man called out. "Can you give us a hand? There are people trapped under here!"

"The Devil you say," Angelus remarked. He put a hand on the man's shoulder in a comradely way. "I wouldn't be gettin' too worked up about it, meself."

Angelus's arm darted around the man's neck, his hand grabbing hold of the jaw. He broke the neck with one quick wrench and let the body slump to the ground.

"You're getting quite good at that," Darla commented.

"I had a good teacher," Angelus said.

The other men had stopped working and now stood with their shovels and picks raised in defense. "Brigands!" one of them cried. "You'll not find us as easy pickings as the bodies of the dead!"

"Living, dead—it's all the same to us," Darla said. Her face transformed into a demonic visage of fangs, yellow eyes and distended bone. She leapt for the throat of the nearest worker.

Angelus just stood back and watched. After all, she deserved to have some fun, too. . . .

A monster with skin like jagged obsidian stalked through the maze of sewers beneath L.A.

Only the bravest Tremblors were chosen to make the journey to the Upper World, with its searing rays of light and chaotic buzz of activity. Baasalt was one of these, a warrior-priest of the deepest level. As he trudged through the tunnel closer and closer to his objective, his thoughts were devout; in order to attune himself to what he sought, he had to be in a meditative, almost trancelike state. It wasn't easy to do while wading through filth, the stench of offal in his nostrils, but Baasalt knew how to keep himself centered. His tribe's history was an oral one, though they spoke mind-to-mind rather than aloud, and he ran through the Sacred Scripts in his mind to help him concentrate.

The Script he recalled now was the oldest of them all: The First Story.

And before Everything, there was the Blood that boiled in the Heart of the World. And the Blood pulsed and surged and forced its way out of the Heart and into the Body of the World, which was frozen and lifeless. The Blood flowed through the Body, seeking to bring it to Life. The cold of the Body mingled with the fire of the Blood, and it slowed and hardened and took new form. This was the Ig, the First Tribe, and they had dominion throughout the Body of the World.

The Ig were not satisfied, and they sent forth

warriors to explore the very Skin of the World. And behold, they found that the Skin was a wretched place. Its surface crawled with all manner of vermin, and the blessed Dark was burned away by horrid Light. Unseen forces howled their way through a vast Emptiness, and all the Ig who ventured there were destroyed. And the Ig turned away from the Skin of the World, and were content to live within.

Baasalt nodded to himself. The First Story was easy; all Tremblors knew it, though not all could remember it as perfectly as a warrior-priest. He stopped before a particular storm drain and extended his tail up as high as it would go; a slit opened on the underside and a pale white tuber unfurled itself from within. It thrust itself between the rusted iron bars of the grate above Baasalt's head and swayed slightly back and forth like the questing head of a worm.

Yes. He could taste the mark that had been put on this place; this was where she lived. The second one, the one that traveled through the Void that Screamed. She was not here now, but Baasalt could wait. His was a patient people.

As he waited, he thought of the Skin-Dweller that he had fought. It had foolishly tried to hunt him, no doubt seeking to—what was the term? "Eat" him. A vile concept, one that had something to do with the reek all around. It had fought harder than he expected, but once it had buried itself in its desperate attempt to survive he had continued on his way and given the matter little thought. In truth, he'd felt a little guilty; slaughtering innocent beasts that were only following their instincts was nothing to be proud of.

As he settled down to wait, he recalled The Second Story.

After many Ages, a new tribe appeared in the Body of the World. They called themselves the Sedim; they were the ghosts of the Ig who had died on the Skin of the World, and they were made of their crushed bones. They were vengeful ghosts, for they blamed the Ig for their deaths, and for abandoning their bones on the Skin of the World.

And so the Ig and the Sedim went to War, and great Convulsions shook the Body of the World. The battle went on for many Ages, and the Body of the World was consumed by War. The dead were so numerous that they clogged the tunnels, and the caves, and the Great Dark Spaces; and all about was death. The

Body of the World was now the Corpse of the World.

But the Soul of the World still lived, and its breath was life and magic. It flowed through the bodies of the fallen, and transformed the dead with its mysterious power. They rose up as a new tribe, and they called themselves the Metamor. And the Metamor went to the Ig, and to the Sedim, and talked to them of the End of War; for the Metamor were Peace-makers.

The Ig and the Sedim saw the wisdom of the Metamor's words, and decided to battle each other no more.

That was the end of the Second Story. Baasalt began the Third.

The Ig, the Sedim, and the Metamor lived in harmony as the Three Tribes. But there came a time when they realized that their numbers were shrinking, for they had no way to reproduce. The Sedim had been born from the bones of the Ig, and the Metamor from the bones of the Ig and the Sedim. Only through Death could there be new Life, and the Three Tribes had forsworn War. Perplexed, they sent a Warrior-Priest to the Heart of the World to ask for advice.

"Great Heart of the World," intoned the

Warrior-Priest, "give us your Wisdom. We wish to live, and yet only Death seems to bring forth new Life. What can we do?"

"In the Belly of the World, only Death can bring forth Life, it is true," said the Heart of the World. "But on the Skin of the World, Life grows in a different way. I can show you this way, but it will require a great Sacrifice of all your people."

"We will do anything," the Warrior-Priest replied.

"Very well. Your tribes must leave their home, and travel throughout the Body of the World. They must not travel together; each must be alone, as one lost. When they have traveled as long and far as they can, when they are far from their tribe and their home, they must lay down in the Earth and sleep."

And the Warrior-Priest returned to the Three Tribes, and told them the Words of the Heart of the World, and they went forth to do as they had been bidden.

And when all members of the Three Tribes had wandered long and far, they lay themselves down in the Earth; and their hearts were sick with loneliness and want. As they slept, their bodies swelled with longing, and grew until they filled all the Body of the

World; and their dreams reached out to the Heart of the World, crying out with their desire.

"Be still, my children," said the Heart of the World, "for I will give you what you long for."

And the dreams of the Three Tribes flowed together and became as one, and from this dream was born the Fourth Tribe. And the body of the Fourth Tribe was made of Ig and Sedim and Metamor, and given power over the Body of the World. And the Heart of the World named them, calling them the Tremblor.

"Thank you, Great Heart of the World, for letting us be born," were the first words of the Tremblor. "But where are our parents?"

"Your parents are now Giants, sleeping within the Body of the World," was the answer. "Indeed, they have become the Body of the World, and you will dwell inside them. They will sleep until they are needed, and on that day they will not waken—but they will dance.

"And the Skin of the World will be laid to waste, and the Tremblor race will grow."

Baasalt smiled to himself with teeth like stalactites. The Third Story had always been his favorite—

and now, The Dance of the Sleeping Giants was nearly upon them . . .

The Skin-Dwellers were soft and wet things and they disgusted him, but they were necessary for the ritual. The blood of four specific creatures from the Skin of the World must be mingled with the Blood of the Heart of the World. So it had always been; so it always would be.

And who was Baasalt to question tradition?

"Kate," Angel said. "Got a minute?"

LAPD detective Kate Lockley looked up from the paperwork she'd been going over. "Angel. Sure, if it's a minute free of forms in triplicate." She brushed a strand of blond hair away from her eyes, and leaned back in her office chair. "What's up?"

Angel sat down in the chair in front of her desk. "I wondered if I could get some help with a case I'm working on."

"Depends. What do you need?"

"Information on missing persons."

"I can probably do that. Who are you looking for?"

Angel hesitated. "It's not a specific person—more likely someone in a particular occupation."

"Sex trade?"

"No, something a little more . . . elemental. Fire, to be exact."

"You're looking for a missing arsonist?"

"Not necessarily. Just someone connected to the field."

Kate frowned and tapped a few keys on her computer. "Well, we *can* search the files by occupation. How about a firefighter?"

"That could be it. When did he disappear?"

"She, Sherlock. And she vanished two weeks ago, right after her shift. Left her car in the parking lot. No leads, no suspects, no known reasons for her to disappear."

"Can I get a name and address?" Angel asked.

"I shouldn't, but—okay. You didn't hear it from me." Kate scrawled the facts down on a piece of paper and handed it over. "Anything else?"

"Water."

"There's a cooler at the end of the hall—"

"No, I mean, have there been any disappearances of people connected with water?"

She gave him a skeptical look. "Connected with water? That could be anyone from a plumber to a surfboard salesman. I mean, I punch in 'fire' and my little search engine does just fine; I punch in 'water,' there's a whole bunch of categories it'll miss. I'd have to go over them personally."

"I'd, uh, really appreciate it if you could. And while you're at it—"

"Let me guess. Missing people connected with air or earth, right?"

"Right. However I can repay you—"

"I want dinner. And wine."

"Dinner is good. Wine is good."

"It'll take me a while to go through the data. I'll call you when I'm done." She looked at him calmly. "Is that it?"

"Well, there was something else I was going to ask you." Angel rubbed the back of his neck awkwardly. "Do you—do you belong to any groups?"

Kate looked at him for a second and arched an eyebrow. "What, you mean like Scientology or EST? Or were you thinking more along the lines of the Supremes?"

"I mean—anything. Church groups, fan clubs, fraternal organizations. Places where you get together with people you have something in common with."

"Well, let me see. There's the Female Detective Appreciation Society that meets Wednesdays, the Police Sewing Circle on the weekends, and of course the Glee Club."

"You belong to a Glee Club?"

She shook her head and sighed. "Angel, I'm kidding. About the only club I belong to is the Police Officers' Association, and I haven't been to a meeting since I joined. Being a detective *and* a woman puts me in a strange sort of limbo; I don't really belong in either locker room, if you know what I mean."

"Yes," Angel said. "I think I do."

Darla killed them all.

When she was done, Angelus applauded. "Bravo!" he said. "Encore!"

Darla gave a little mock bow. "I'm glad you approve. But now that the fires have finally burned themselves out, men like this will become more common; I fear your own little drama will soon have to close."

Angelus sighed. "Ah, you're right, of course. At least they did most of the work before you sent them to their great reward."

The trapdoor had almost been cleared. Angelus threw aside the last few chunks of rubble, leaving only a single oak beam blocking the way. "Maria!" he called down. "Are you still there?"

Silence.

"Dead?" Darla said. "Wouldn't that be a shame . . ."

"I think not," Angelus said. "I fear my dear Maria has figured out my little game, and she doesn't want to play anymore. Not that she has a choice . . .

"Maria! I know you can hear me, darlin'. And in a moment, you'll see my face. Isn't that *grand?*"

". . . go away . . ."

Angelus laughed. "Oh, have we had a change of heart? Six days down in the dark, and suddenly I'm not good enough for you. Whatever brought *this* on?"

". . . Where's Ernesto? I want to talk to Ernesto."

Angelus glanced down at the body of the man whose neck he'd snapped. "Ernesto, is it? He's . . . taking a break."

"You killed him." She sounded detached.

"Actually, it's worse than that," Angelus said. "He was never real. It was just me, pretending, the whole time. Just like you were pretending about Francesco and Estrellita, weren't you? They were dead from the beginning. You just thought I might work a little harder for three survivors than one."

"You're the Devil." She might have been talking about the weather for all the emotion in her voice.

"No, but I've played cards with him once or twice," Angelus said cheerfully. "He's not as good at it as you might think. Me, though—when I play, I never lose."

"Go away. You'll never have my soul."

"Your soul? Dear me, I'm not interested in such a

paltry little item as that. Really, I just want you for your *mind*."

He grabbed hold of the oaken beam and heaved it aside. "Ready or not, here I come," he said with a grin.

He pulled the trapdoor open.

CHAPTER FOUR

"So here's what I'm thinkin'," Doyle said. He and Angel were driving through East L.A. "These Tremblor guys—they can't be the brightest bulbs on the Christmas tree, intellectually speakin'."

"How's that?"

"Well, they're made outta rock, right? So, their *brains* are made outta rock."

"I'm not following."

"Do I gotta draw you a picture? Rocks in the head. That's like, universally known as a metaphor for being simple."

"That's kind of speciest of you, don't you think?"

"Kinda *what*?"

"Speciest. Attributing one stereotypical quality to a species as a whole."

"Like sayin' all vampires drink blood, for instance?"

Angel frowned. "That's *exactly* what I mean. I drink coffee, I can appreciate a good single-malt as much as you—but all you remember is type A, O, or AB negative."

"All right, all right, point taken. A little touchy today, are we?"

"I don't talk in a bad Transylvanian accent, either."

"I said all right! Geez, *someone* woke up on the wrong side of the coffin today."

"Very funny. Maybe I should wear a cape."

"Depends. Are you still talkin' Dracula, or have we moved on to Batman?"

"We're here." Angel pulled over and parked. Across the street, neon beer signs lit up the window of a small bar.

"Okay, tell y'what. Since I've obviously offended your sensibilities by implyin' you're nothin' but a bloodsuckin' freak—"

"You never said *freak*—"

"—let me make it up t'you by buyin' you a shot of the finest Scotch this establishment has t'offer."

They got out of the car. "That should set you back all of two dollars," Angel said, looking the place up and down. The faded, peeling sign read CHICO'S PLACE. Broken glass sparkled on the sidewalk around the entrance, a beat-up metal door.

Inside, the place was about as bad as Angel had

expected. A long bar down one side, a row of booths down the other. Cracked red Naugahyde upholstery and scarred Formica tables. Most of the light came from the beer signs. There was a middle-aged Latina behind the bar, and three regulars huddled together at one end of it. Angel could tell they were regulars simply by their body language; "I've been here for a long time," their posture said. "And I'm not going anywhere else, anytime soon."

They slid into a booth where they could watch the door. Doyle ordered two Scotches from the bartender.

"So this is where Graedeker hangs out?" Angel asked.

"Sometimes. He can be a hard man t'track down. Usually, *he* finds *you.*"

"How does that work?"

Doyle shrugged. "It's kinda uncanny, actually. Let's say you're a demon who's down on your luck. Maybe you picked the wrong horse, or you're behind on a couple alimony payments to the ol' succubus. Up sidles this guy who seems t'know about your troubles. 'Maybe I can help you out,' he says. 'I'd be willing to lend you a little cash, as long as you got something to put up as collateral.' Now, we're not talkin' stereos or wristwatches, here; he's strictly interested in supernatural items."

"And if the demon defaults on the loan, he keeps the item."

"Right. He's a pawnbroker, more or less. Thing is, sometimes gettin' your property back is a little more difficult than pawning it off in the first place."

"He doesn't like to return things?"

The bartender arrived with their drinks. Doyle checked his pockets and looked sheepish. Angel paid her.

"It's not so much that," Doyle continued. "It's just that he can be hard to find. You ever watch *The Twilight Zone?*"

"I prefer books to television."

"Yeah, well, there's this episode with an old curio shop, right? And this guy goes in there and winds up buying a magic bottle, and when he opens the bottle it changes him into Adolf Hitler."

"Now I know why I don't watch television."

"Okay, maybe I got a few of the details wrong, but the important thing is, when he goes back to the shop to get a refund, it's not there anymore."

A thoughtful look crossed Angel's face, but he didn't say anything.

"So anyway—"

"I'm still trying to picture Hitler asking for a refund," Angel said.

Doyle took a sip of his Scotch and tried not to wince. "Yeah, well, this idea of a disappearing store,

I've seen the notion used a couple times. Movies, TV shows. Musta been where Graedeker picked it up."

"He has a disappearing pawnshop?"

"Not exactly. He's got a semitrailer he keeps his goods in; calls it the Devil's Tulips. Lives in a sleeper compartment in the back of the rig. Moves it around a lot."

"Like the old Medicine shows," Angel mused. "Used to be popular on the Western frontier. Sell you anything from Eternal Youth Elixir to magic beans."

"If you're more comfortable with an analogy from the last century instead of this one, fine—but this guy deals only with the real goods. And if the Serpentene are half the businessmen they claim t'be, Graedeker should know all about 'em."

"The last century . . . that's the problem."

"Good God, this Scotch is terrible. I need another one." Doyle signaled the bartender.

"My frame of reference, my roots—they're all in the last two centuries, not this one." Angel took a drink of Scotch and grimaced.

"So?"

"So it's affecting my work. A detective has to be able to blend in, not stick out."

"You seem to be doin' pretty well so far, detective-wise."

"I just don't feel like I'm . . . *integrated*."

"Integrated? At the risk of soundin' like a speciest, bein' . . . *daylight-challenged* doesn't exactly put you in the Typical American category. But that's not what this is really about, is it?"

"I'm just saying—"

"You're just saying you don't fit in. You don't belong. Welcome to the club, pal." Doyle raised his drink, then stopped and frowned. "Wait. If you're in a club, then you *do* belong. You know, it sounded a lot better in my head."

"All right, it's not being different that bothers me," Angel admitted. "I've been a vampire for almost two and a half centuries. I've gotten used to that. It's knowing there's *no one* else like me. I'm a species of one, Doyle."

"Well, this *is* the great meltin' pot of the world. Sweet land of liberty. If you can make it here you can make it anywhere."

"You're not going to start singing, are you?"

"It's within the realm of possibility . . ."

The first thing Angelus saw was a crucifix.

He wasn't surprised. It was, after all, a church—and Maria already thought he was the Devil. If she had any doubts, they'd soon be gone . . .

The hand holding the crucifix was bloodstained, grimy and shaking. The shaft of moonlight coming through the trapdoor fell directly on the cross, throwing off glints of silver that stabbed into Angelus's eyes like daggers. He fought the instinctive urge to hiss and back away, and smiled instead. The pain of the cross could be endured; all it took was will power.

"Now, darlin'," he said softly. "You don't think I'm afraid of a little trinket like that, do you? All *that* does is make me nostalgic."

"Keep back, keep back . . ."

"I was there when they nailed him up, you know." Angelus took one slow step forward. It was like walking against a strong wind . . . but one that was faltering.

One that was dying.

"It's takin' every ounce of strength you have just to hold that little thing up, isn't it? And I just tossed an oaken beam aside like it was a piece of firewood. Do you really think you stand a chance against me?"

"Go *away* . . ."

"I'm not goin' anywhere. Y'see, I've developed these feelin's for you . . . feelin's I can't quite describe. *Passionate* feelin's. Somewhere between love and murder, between the smell of a rose and the blood drippin' off its thorns.

"I want your heart, darlin'. And I *mean* that . . ."

Then he just stood there, in the dark.

And waited for her arm to fall.

❖   ❖   ❖

"You ever belong to any groups?" Angel asked. He was still nursing his first drink.

"Me?" said Doyle. "Nah. I mean, there's a number of twelve-step programs that would love to have me, but so far, I've just said no. T'the programs, that is."

"I figured. You don't slow down on the Scotch, pretty soon you'll be asking for a ride to Wendy's."

"Me, pull a Cordelia? Angel, come *on*. I've had more to drink before breakfast. Or *for* breakfast, for that matter."

"As long as you can deal with Graedeker."

"Not a problem." Doyle took another drink. "You know, this stuff really improves once your tongue goes numb. Hey, I just remembered somethin', a group I *did* belong to. Geez, I haven't thought about those guys in years."

"What group was it?"

"The Justice Fighters. We were superheroes."

Angel raised his eyebrows. "Superheroes."

"Oh, sure. Fought crime in my basement, mainly. You know, for a middle-class neighborhood, my basement was surprisingly seedy."

Angel smiled. "How old were you?"

"Around eight. When we weren't battlin' the forces of darkness, we lay around and read each other's comic books. I had a pretty impressive collection myself."

"Another twentieth-century art form that's passed me by."

"That's a shame; some of those guys were really good. Take Jack Kirby, for instance. He and Stan Lee practically invented modern-day comics."

"Stanley who?"

"Stan *Lee*. They created Spiderman, the Fantastic Four, the Incredible Hulk . . ."

"Any of them vampires?"

"Well, no—"

"Didn't think so."

"There was this one character called the Demon, though, somethin' Kirby came up with on his own. Regular-lookin' guy most o' the time. But when he recites this spell, he transforms into a creature from the Pit. Bright yellow skin, claws, horns, fins where his ears should be. Ugly bastard. Didn't have a lot of friends." Doyle stared down at his drink, swirling the ice cubes around slowly with one finger.

"Yeah? He your favorite?"

Doyle looked up. "What? Nah, he dressed weird and talked funny. My personal favorite was Wonder Woman, which eventually got me kicked out of the Justice Fighters and gave me a lifelong fetish for star-spangled underwear. And lassos that glow in the dark."

The silver crucifix, glinting in the moonlight . . .

Angel shook his head and took a slug of Scotch.

"Somethin' the matter, pal? You looked a little more broody than usual for a second."

"You know how there's something you haven't thought of in decades, and suddenly it just . . . rises up in your mind? And then you can't stop thinking about it?"

"I don't know about the decades part, but—yeah, sure. I take it this isn't an old pop song we're talkin' about?"

"No. It was something I did, a long time ago. Shortly after I became a vampire. Something horrible." Angel finished his Scotch in a single drink. "It happened in Portugal, after a big earthquake destroyed most of Lisbon."

"I can see how the current case might stir up a few memories. You want t'talk about it?"

"Not really. It was . . . monstrous. Maybe not the worst thing I ever did, but definitely in the top ten. It was my first real exploration of psychological torture as opposed to the physical kind, and I took to it like a duck to water. I don't think you want to hear the details—especially not what I did at the end."

"Angel, you're still a genius at psychological torture—y'just switched to the self-inflicted variety. You're like the Jedi master of guilt."

"I know, I know. It's just that all this talking about

groups has gotten me to thinking . . . maybe I *shouldn't* belong anywhere."

"Why? Because y'don't deserve to? Angel, everyone deserves a little joy—"

"Doyle, for me a little joy equals a lot of mass murder."

"Oh. Right." Doyle nodded. "Forgot about that whole a-single-moment-of-true-happiness-and-you-lose-your-soul-again business. Gypsy curses are a bitch, aren't they . . ."

Angel looked around and sighed. "It's almost closing time. I don't think he's going to show."

"I think you're right. Just let me hit the john and we're outta here."

"I'll wait in the car."

Angel was just about to unlock his door when he heard them. Four young men, approaching from the shadows. Baggy jeans, plaid shirts, expensive sneakers. Their colors marked them as Bloods.

"Nice ride," the shortest gang member said. One glance at his eyes told Angel he was the leader.

Angel slipped his keys back into his pocket. "Thanks—but my ex-wife dumped a load of rotting fish in it during the divorce, and I still can't get the smell out."

"The only thing *I* smell is B.S.," the largest one said. His arms could have been an ad for a prison gym.

"Give it up," the leader said. Suddenly there was a gun in his hand.

Angel sighed. "Great. Now I'm going to get shot. I *hate* getting shot. It hurts, you know? And it puts holes in my shirts."

"You got a strange set a priorities for a dead man. The keys, if you please."

The front door of the bar banged closed as Doyle left. He froze when he saw the scene across the street—and the short one's eyes flickered to him for just a second.

Angel grabbed the gunman's arm, clamping one hand between his elbow and his shoulder and one over the top of his gun hand. He bent the arm back and suddenly the gangbanger found his own pistol jammed under his chin.

"Hold it," Angel said.

Two of the others pulled guns of their own. One was aimed at Angel, while the big guy covered Doyle.

"Let him go or I'll drop your friend," the big guy growled.

"With that?" Angel said calmly. "I don't think so. Snub-nose thirty-eight isn't much good past thirty feet, and he's at least forty feet away. I doubt you could hit him once out of a full clip."

"I may be forty feet away but I can hear you just fine!" Doyle said nervously. "Some of us aren't quite as lead-resistant as others, you know—"

"Give it up," the leader hissed.

"Now, all I have to do to turn your friend's brains into a colorful fountain is twitch," Angel continued. "And considering that he's between me and you, we're going to get his brains all over both of us. Now, that doesn't bother me because I know an *excellent* dry-cleaner, but maybe it's an experience you don't really want to go through."

The one without a gun was looking more and more nervous. His shaved head gleamed under the streetlights. "Hey, maybe we should just go, huh?"

"You cap him, we cap you," the big one said. "Your friend might get away, but that ain't gonna do *you* a whole lot of good, you know?"

"True," Angel admitted. "Except for one thing."

"Which is?"

Angel let the vampiric persona he normally kept suppressed rise to the surface.

His irises went from black to bright yellow. The ridge of bone over his eyes thickened. He grinned at them with a mouth full of teeth that had just gotten a lot longer and sharper.

"Which is the fact that bullets only annoy me. And when I'm annoyed, I rip people's throats out. You'd be amazed what a stress-reliever it is . . ."

The gangbangers met his gaze. They all lowered their weapons.

"Shit," the big one said. "You a *vampire*." He sounded disgusted.

"Uh—well, yeah," Angel said.

"Why didn' you say so, homes? We got a treaty with the vamps around here. They don' feed on Bloods, we don' drag their pale asses out inta the sunlight. We cool." He lowered his gun, and the others did the same.

"Right," Angel said. He released his grip on the leader, who glared at him but stepped back.

"Watch your ass around here, though," the big one said. "Lotta demons don' respect our turf. Can't be responsible if one of 'em whacks you."

"I'll . . . be careful," Angel said. "Thanks."

"No prob. Later, fangs." They strode off down the sidewalk.

Doyle walked up to the car. "Y'know," he said, staring after the departing Bloods, "just when I think L.A. can't get any weirder . . ."

"Kate won't have the breakdown on other possible victims for me until tomorrow," Angel said. "So all we have to work with is the attack on the Serpentene woman—and this."

"A firehouse," Doyle said. They were parked across the street from it. "Where this woman Fisca worked. You think she was number one on the Tremblors' shoppin' list?"

"Maybe," Angel said. "According to Kate, she vanished sometime between getting off work and walking to her car, which was parked in the lot right next to the hall. I thought we might have a look around."

They got out of the car and crossed the street. The parking lot was well-lit, with spots along one brick wall marked RESERVED FOR MEMBERS OF THE FIRE DEPARTMENT.

"Not a lot of places t'hide," Doyle observed. "Coulda been between two vehicles, I suppose."

"Or below one," Angel said. "These are subterranean creatures, after all . . ." He walked down to the end of the parking lot. "Look at this," he said.

Doyle joined him. "New asphalt. Like the ground was dug up and paved over again."

"The city repairs sinkholes all the time. If this was being worked on the night Fisca disappeared, the ground could have been exposed."

"And one of our rocky friends coulda been just below the surface." Doyle nodded. "Okay, but that still leaves a few questions. Like, how does the Tremblor know his victim is an actual firefighter and not someone who just parked here? For that matter, how does he know *anything* while he's underground? Does he poke his head up from time to time like a gopher?"

"I don't know," Angel admitted. "I didn't get that good a look at the one that attacked me. It could have had some special kind of sensory organs that weren't obvious."

"Let's try and re-create the situation," Doyle suggested. "The kidnapping, I mean, not your premature burial. Kinda put ourselves in the Quake demon's place, try and figure out what he was thinkin'."

"All right. Well, the Tremblor had to have been waiting for his victim, maybe for some time—"

"Okay. So he's been waiting' here awhile. He's gettin' jumpy, nervous."

"Maybe," Angel said. He leaned against the wall and crossed his arms.

Doyle started pacing back and forth. "He's all charged up with earthquake energy, right? Like that whammy he used on you. He's practically *vibratin'*. He's ready and rarin' to go . . ."

Baasalt waited.

Waiting did not bother him. He reckoned time by a geologic clock; he was older than most countries. Waiting was only stillness, and stillness to a Tremblor was like sunshine to a lizard.

Not that it was *true* stillness. The filth still flowed past his knees, sloshing and gurgling its way down the tunnel; rats rustled and squeaked and gnawed at garbage; and that was just within the tunnel itself.

Outside was pandemonium.

Giant metal bugs roared around at insane speeds. Footsteps clattered on concrete. Voices yammered, dogs barked, birds shrieked. At least it was no longer the period called "day," though that would come again soon enough.

Baasalt's world was largely a silent one. Even the murmur of underground rivers did not reach his realm. Years sometimes passed between one audible sound and another; his people communicated directly from mind to mind.

How he missed it . . .

"And then," Doyle said, "Fresca comes out."

"Fisca."

"Yeah, yeah. But what if Mr. Shake-and-Quake screws up? Could be all us surface types look the same to him; moles and worms aren't exactly known for their great eyesight . . ."

Baasalt's pale white sensory tuber quivered slightly. It was actually a separate organism, a kind of symbiotic fungus that would only grow in one environment: the tail slit of Tremblor warrior-priests. It was a delicate and sensitive instrument, able to detect the tinest amount of any chemical compound and convey that information to its host. To Baasalt's sensory tuber, identical twins were about as similar as black and white.

"So it's not even the right person," Doyle continued. "But the Quake demon don't know that. It probably just hears footsteps, knockin' on its roof. It's not too bright, so it doesn't waste a lot of time thinkin'. It wants some *action*. It erupts outta the ground," Doyle said, throwing his arms in the air. "Right in front of her, probably. She turns to run, but it's too fast. It grabs her from behind . . ."

Angel sighed.

The one he had been seeking drew near.

He could taste her, molecule by molecule. The scent of her perfume, her clothes, her hair, all these were just distractions. It was the other, secondary essences that clung to her that told him she was one of the Four.

A complex petrochemical tang that spoke of metal birds screaming through the Void. A faint miasma of elements that underlaid that, the kind of collective stink produced by a group of Skin Dwellers trapped together for a short period of time. A subtle wrongness in her biology that indicated a confused internal clock.

More important was her lifeline, an energy signature that ran through time the way light traveled through space, and just as visible to Baasalt. Its regularity told him that she was not merely a sometimes air-traveler; it was her profession. She was connected to the Void that Screamed as surely as he was connected to the Body of the World.

He shuddered, trying not to think about it. He would have to proceed carefully with this one.

The flower growing out of the storm drain was the oddest one Sarah Clark had ever seen.

The stalk was pale white, but that was practically normal compared to the bloom. It looked like—well, like a volcano, Sarah supposed. It had a cone that was jet-black, with red edging around the top that suggested molten rock, and incredibly long, scarlet stamens that projected almost two feet into the air from the top of the cone, the ends curving in gentle arcs like lava falling back to earth after shooting out of the ground.

Actually, it looked more like a mushroom, but not any mushroom Sarah had ever seen. And mushrooms didn't *have* stamens, did they? They gave off spores, not pollen.

And they didn't smell like summer camp.

Sarah stopped dead. Her job as a flight attendant took her all over the world, and her nose had encountered many an unusual aroma: she had wandered around open-air bazaars in Morocco, strolled past cooking stalls in Hong Kong, stuck her head in spice shops in the Philippines. She loved the sense of the exotic strange smells induced.

But there was something to be said for the familiar, too, especially for those smells that called up memories. What she was smelling now was something from her twelfth year, the last year she went to summer camp. She remembered it as a haven, of a place removed from the problems of her everyday life; it was the last summer of her childhood, and she'd spent it having fun and making friends. She learned important things, not about archery or swimming or canoeing, but the things young girls always discuss: getting your first period. How to kiss a boy. Trying beer or a cigarette to see what all the fuss was about. Training bras and makeup.

And somehow, even from twenty feet away, that was what this flower smelled like. The sweet scent of pine trees, underlaid with that musty smell her cabin had. That cheap perfume Ellen

Fingerhoff had spilled. The smell of warm, weathered wood and creosote that rose off the dock while she was sunbathing. The slightly marshy aroma of the lake. And wood smoke, of course . . .

She approached the flower with a half-smile on her face. As she got closer to the storm drain it was growing out of, she saw that the sewer grate was missing, leaving a dark, empty hole. Empty except for an unusual flower, swaying slightly back and forth.

Sarah put her face close to the bloom, closed her eyes and inhaled.

And fell, backward, through time.

"Come *on*," an excited voice yelled. "Look at this!"

Sarah opened her eyes and straightened up. *Cool-looking flower*, she thought. *Doesn't have much of a smell, though.*

Her best friend, Cindy Lillinett, was standing beside what looked like—a cave! It had been covered up by bushes, but Cindy had pulled them aside. "Isn't this great?" Cindy asked her. "I bet no one's been in here for a hundred years!"

Sarah grinned and ran over. "But it's so close to the camp. You think maybe this is where the counselors come to make out or something?"

"Maybe," Cindy said. "Let's go inside."

"You first," Sarah said.

Cindy smiled and said, "Chicken?" then ducked into the cave.

Sarah was right behind her.

"Would you like a trampoline?" Angel asked.

"Excuse me?" Doyle said.

"To help you make those great leaps of logic."

"And I suppose you can do better?"

"Well, let's see. First of all, the Tremblors have already attacked a firefighter and someone who lives underground—two for two in terms of what they're after. That suggests they know what they're doing. Second, the one I fought waited until I stumbled upon it. That plus this attack suggests waiting is part of the Tremblor's natural strategy. And even though the Tremblor that attacked me was fairly quick, I can't see something made of rock having an impatient personality. . . ."

Angel began walking back toward the car. "The firehouse is staffed twenty-four hours a day, and right next door; if something erupted out of the earth and grabbed her, she'd at least have time to scream. No one heard a thing."

"So what *did* happen?" Doyle asked, following him.

"I don't know. Maybe it drugged her, hypnotized

her or something. We don't have enough information at this point to tell."

They got into the car. "Where to?" Doyle asked.

"Fisca's apartment. Maybe the victims are linked together in another way, one that could help us figure out who's next."

Baasalt led the female by the hand. She came willingly, a happy smile on her face. The spores emitted by the sensory tuber were psychoactive in a very special way—they took their victim back to his or her happiest time, a time when they were safe and trusting. Baasalt could clearly see the difference in her lifeline; her body was here, but her mind had cast itself backward. Such a state made her extremely suggestible—Baasalt didn't even have to speak to her mind. He simply made a beckoning gesture with his hand, and her own thoughts filled in the details.

He was glad it had been easy. One never knew what would happen when dealing with the Void, or those who lived in it.

"So this is where she lived," Doyle said.

The apartment was spacious and well-furnished; apparently L.A. firefighters made decent wages. Security was less than impressive, though—

Doyle had managed to pick the lock in under a minute.

Angel glanced around. Bookshelves, framed art posters, leather couch with matching chair. A television, a stereo, a rack of CDs and videotapes. A coffee table with a few magazines on it. Nothing that jumped out and said, "I'm going to be kidnapped by underground monsters!"

"Hey, you think she'll mind if I eat this?" Doyle said, his head in the refrigerator. "As an advance thank-you for rescuin' her, and all."

Angel walked into the bedroom. The double bed was unmade, heaps of clothes lying on the floor.

There was a computer on a desk against one wall; he pulled out the chair, sat down and turned on the power.

It didn't seem to be encrypted in any way, so he had a look through her files. She was working on a novel, had a stash of Victorian erotic literature and a collection of flight simulator games. Angel found her address list and scanned through it.

The name was near the end, of course. It caught Angel's eye as he scrolled past, and he immediately stopped and backed up.

"Doyle," he called out. "I think I've found something."

Doyle walked in, a half-eaten submarine sandwich in one hand and a beer in the other. "Yeah? What's that?"

"A name," Angel said. "A very familiar name."

He pointed at the screen. It was two names, actually.

Wolfram and Hart.

CHAPTER FIVE

Wolfram and Hart was a name Angel knew well. They were an L.A. law firm, one whose clientele leaned heavily toward the demonic—in the worst sense of the word. He'd faced off against them before, and barely survived the experience.

By the time Angel and Doyle were done searching the apartment, it was almost dawn; they found nothing else that seemed important. They drove back to the office, and Angel retired to his own place downstairs to get some sleep.

It was a long time coming. He tried to concentrate on the case, but his mind kept drifting back to Lisbon, back to the ruins of the church, back to Maria.

Back to what he finally imposed on her.

❖   ❖   ❖

"Morning, Angel," Cordelia called out as he stepped off the freight elevator. "Or afternoon, I guess. There's coffee."

"Coffee is good," Angel muttered, walking into the office. He poured himself a cup. "Where's Doyle?"

"Out getting lunch, for those of us who chew our food."

Angel sank into an office chair, but didn't reply.

"What, is that like a disgusting concept to you now? Putting stuff in your mouth and chomping on it until it's all mushy and mixed together, then swallowing—euuw, suddenly I'm not hungry anymore. Thanks a lot."

"Sorry. I didn't sleep well."

"Doyle says you found a connection to Wolfram and Hart. What *is* it with those creeps—are they trying to corner the market on evil or something?"

"Or something," Angel agreed. "I don't know how they're involved yet—they were in one of the victims' address files."

"Oh, and that cop lady dropped by with some information. She said to give you this." Cordelia picked up an envelope and handed it to Angel.

The front door opened and Doyle came in, a brown paper bag under one arm. "I see the big guy's up. Cordy, I hope tandoori's okay."

"You can have mine. Mr. Sunshine here just spoiled my appetite."

Doyle set the paper bag down on the desk. "What's in the envelope?"

"Something from Kate." Angel opened it up and took out a thick sheaf of paper. "Looks like a printout on missing persons. She's listed all the ones in the last six months that might be Tremblor victims."

"Not that you told her that," Cordelia said.

"Of course not."

"So what *did* you tell her?" Doyle asked, unpacking the contents of the paper bag.

"Just that it was a case I was working on," Angel said, studying the printout.

"Pretty big favor for such a vague reason," Doyle commented.

"She must be a very nice person," Cordelia said.

"Just likes to help people," Doyle agreed.

"For absolutely *no* reward, of course."

"Other than a feelin' of mutual self-respect for a fellow detective."

"That's *just* what I was going to say."

Angel sighed and put down the printout. "Okay, okay. I promised I'd take her out for dinner."

"As long as you don't *have* her for dinner," Cordelia said. "But you wouldn't do that unless you turned evil, and that wouldn't happen unless you experienced actual happiness, which is usually an *après*-dinner kind of thing."

"Unless the appetizers are *really* outstandin'." Doyle opened a foil container and the smell of curry wafted out.

"By the way—isn't this a cool outfit?" Cordelia extended her arms and spun around. The dress was tight and black and had holes cut in unusual places.

"Very nice."

"And expensive," Doyle added.

"I take it Maureen paid for the clothes?" Angel asked.

"She insisted. Who was I to say no? She could have gone all snaky on me or something."

"I'm sure you held out as long as you could. How did things go otherwise?"

"Oh, we had a great time. Well, there *was* that ugly incident with the hamster at the pet store, but she said her blood sugar was low."

"She ate a hamster?" Doyle said. He paused with a forkful of curry halfway to his mouth.

"You are *so* gullible. Honestly, Angel, she was perfectly normal. We got along great, and she's really nice. I mean, if *I* had as much money as she did, no *way* I'd hang with someone like me. Not until I'd done a few movies, anyway."

"That . . . almost made sense," Angel said. "But

I'd still like to know a little more about all the Serpentene."

"I'm gonna take another shot at findin' Graedeker on my own," Doyle said. "Could be he's got some way of sensin' when somebody's actually down on their luck, as opposed t'just lookin' t'talk to him."

"You're down on your luck?" Angel asked.

"I will be once I blow my rent money at the track."

"Again, very close to actual sense," Angel said. "Shopping and gambling, two of the pillars of detective work. Myself, I think I'm going to try something unusual."

"And what would that be?" Doyle asked around a mouthful of tandoori.

"Looking for clues. You may have heard the phrase at some point . . ."

Angel spent the afternoon in his office, poring over Kate's printout. She'd scrawled *Good Luck* across the top, and as he looked through the reports he saw why.

The problem was that the parameters he'd given her—people connected to air, earth, or water—were too broad. Did someone who lived on Granite Street count as someone close to earth? Was a washing-machine repairman close to water? It was all too subjective.

He finally laid out a map of L.A. on the floor and stuck a red pin where Fisca had been taken. It didn't really accomplish much, but it made him feel like a detective.

The phone rang in the outer office. Cordelia answered.

"Hello, Angel Investigations—we help the helpless. Yes, he's here. Just a sec. Angel! It's Kate."

He picked up his phone. "Yes?"

"Angel. Something just came in you might be interested in: a flight attendant's gone missing, according to her roommate. No signs of foul play or reasons for her to disappear."

"Like Fisca. Where was she last seen?"

"She took a cab from the airport to her apartment. Never made it inside."

He wrote down the name and address Kate gave him, thanked her and hung up.

A flight attendant and a firefighter. He thought he saw the glimmer of a pattern—both of them helped people, though in very different ways. Both were put in actual danger by the element they worked with.

He took another red pin and stuck it into the map where the flight attendant had vanished. *Nothing unusual between the two points—but let's pretend they're two points of a box. If all the sides are the same length, then the third and fourth points would fall here . . . and here.*

The third point didn't mean anything to Angel—
but the fourth point did. He tapped the spot with
his finger, and smiled. "Gotcha," he said.

We require the location of the next sacrifice,
Baasalt thought.

He was not merely ruminating to himself. He was
in telepathic contact with a Skin-Dweller, one who
was assisting the Tremblors in their quest. His name
was Rome.

We have requirements of our own, Rome thought
back. *The Serpentene have still not been persuaded.*

Being in mental contact with a Skin-Dweller was
distasteful to Baasalt; it was like being immersed in
something wet and twitching. It produced an
uncomfortable feeling that he could only define as
wanting-this-to-be-over. There was no word for
impatience in Baasalt's language. *Do you wish us to
produce another tremor?*

No, I think something more direct is called for . . .

The spot Angel had zeroed in on was on the
beach, right by a lifeguard station. Since all the
attacks had been at night and in secluded areas,
Angel reasoned the Tremblors would target a lifeguard somewhere between work and home.

Two lifeguards were stationed at the post during
the day. Angel planned for him and Doyle to

shadow them after their shifts, then keep an eye on where they lived.

"I've also ordered some special equipment that should be effective against the Tremblors," Angel said. "It'll be ready in a day or so."

Doyle nodded. "Right. So if a big nasty demon busts out of the ground, I'll have just what I need t'take care of the bugger."

"You'll have your cell phone. You'll call me."

"Glad t'see we're on the same page."

Angel got up and slipped on his leather trenchcoat. "Any luck with Graedeker?"

"Well, phase one of the plan went beautifully."

"You lost all your money at the track."

"Yep. I'm still workin' on phase two."

Cordelia stuck her head in. "Guys—bad news. Galvin just called. There's been another attack at Appletree."

"We're on our way."

"Anybody hurt?" Angel asked.

"Thankfully, no," Galvin said. He shook his head ruefully. "Not physically, anyway."

He sat amidst the wreckage of his living room. The grand piano was nothing but splinters and strings, the Picasso, the Rembrandt and the Van Gogh were tatters of ripped canvas. The teak bar had deep gouges in its surface—it looked like it had been used as a scratching post by angry bears. The air was full of the smell of fine Scotch. Not a single bottle had survived.

"This is a tragedy, a real tragedy," Doyle said. He inhaled deeply, and his eyes glistened.

"Oh, they're just things," Galvin said. He smiled, but his eyes were sad. "They can be replaced. What they really destroyed was our sense of security."

Angel eyed the gaping hole in one wall. Dirt spilled out from the edges of the dark tunnel that lay beyond. "You said there were three of them?"

"Yes. They came through in three different apartments. Ignored the residents, but ruined as much of the furnishings as they could. Never said a word."

Angel frowned. "This doesn't quite fit."

"How d'you mean?" Doyle asked.

"Tremors I can see; that's natural for these demons. And grabbing a sacrifice for their ritual makes sense, too. But this—this is terrorism."

Galvin shrugged. "They hate us, that seems plain. Why, I don't know."

"Well, I could try following these tunnels again," Angel said. "But it's too easy for them to set ambushes, or simply collapse the tunnels. I'd rather not deal with them on their own turf, not without a plan."

"What would you suggest we do?" Galvin asked

quietly. "They've proved they can invade us at any time they want."

"I know it's difficult, but I'd suggest you relocate temporarily. Just until this is over—"

"No," Galvin said, shaking his head emphatically. "We won't be driven out of our homes! We were exiled once, and we swore we'd never let it happen again. If we have to stay here under siege, then so be it."

Angel sighed. "I can't protect you here. Like you said, they can attack at any time, from any direction. Even if you armor-plate the walls, they can bring the whole building down on top of you."

"Then you'll just have to stop them before they do, won't you?"

"Nice of Galvin to lend us some wheels," Doyle said. "This Mercedes is top o' the line. Leather interior, CD player, built-in hands-free cell phone—I could get used t'this."

"It's just for the stakeout," Angel's voice said from the speaker. "Don't touch anything. Or spill anything."

"Loosen up, boss," Doyle said. He was parked in the beach lot, a discreet distance from the lifeguard station. "Sun's almost down. You can come out and play soon."

Angel was actually parked in the same lot, a few

cars away. His convertible had been made sunproof through heavy tinting of the windows. "Good. I feel like I'm in an aquarium."

Doyle adjusted the air conditioning. "It's not too warm over there, is it?"

"I'm fine."

"Good, good." Doyle slipped in a CD. He hummed along to the latest Smashing Pumpkins.

"Doyle, I told you not to touch anything."

"Relax, I brought along my own music. That's my, uh, Walkman you hear."

"If you're listening to a Walkman, then how can you hear me?"

"All right, all right." He turned down the stereo. "You know what your problem is? You have an overdeveloped sense of guilt."

"Not overdeveloped—perfected. Took me a long time, but I think I finally got the formula just right."

"Well, it's hard to argue with a century of angst-ridden brooding, but I'll take a crack at it. You and me, Angel, we're different sides of the coin; you wallow in blamin' yourself, while I'm as guilt-free as no-fat potato chips. Without the monosodium gluta-mate."

"Okay, genius. What's your secret?"

Doyle leaned his seat back to a more comfortable position. "It's a matter of conditionin'. Take drinkin', for instance; y'know that terrible feelin' of shame y'get after a night of boozin' it up? Even if you haven't done anythin' bad, you feel like you owe the world an apology?'

"Usually I did."

"Well—mass murder notwithstandin'—that feelin' is an illusion. See, alcohol suppresses inhibitions, right? And guilt is just the stick our inhibitions whack us with when we get outta line. So when our inhibitions get suppressed, so does our guilt. Y'with me?"

"So far."

"Now, when y'sober up, all your inhibitions come back. But because they were pushed down, they spring back, even stronger, along with the guilt. You get this psychological backlash, and automatically feel guilty even if you don't deserve to."

"And you deal with this how?"

"Usually I take another drink. Works wonders."

"Yeah, well, I drank for a hundred years, and felt guilty for the hundred years after that," Angel said.

"Wow. That's gotta be the worst hangover in history."

"I wasn't talking about booze."

"Uh, yeah. O'course not . . ."

"Sure," Cordelia said. "Angel and Doyle get to babysit lifeguards—lifeguards with their sun-bronzed, athletic bodies and tiny, stylish swimsuits—and I get to play detective."

She was standing in the hallway of a motel, holding a clipboard and talking to herself. Angel had sent her to see if she could find any connection between Wolfram and Hart and the vanished flight attendant; this was where the woman had lived.

Okay, I can do this, Cordelia thought. She tried to feel the role, to become the person she was pretending to be, just like she'd read in all those books on acting. Well, skimmed, anyway.

All Cordelia had ever really wanted was for things to be easy. For a long time, they *had* been easy, and she'd taken them for granted. She was pretty, she was popular, she was rich . . . and then things had started going wrong. Weird monsters had started popping up like zits on a teenage boy. She'd fallen for a total loser . . . and then fell for real, on a metal spike that had gone right through her. The IRS had nailed her father for income tax evasion, and suddenly she wasn't rich anymore. Or her parents weren't, which was the same thing.

And then high school had ended.

She missed it. Despite Buffy, despite Xander, despite all the monsters . . . in high school, she'd been on top. She knew how things worked. Now she was out in the real world, and being pretty just wasn't enough, so she'd done the only thing that made sense: she'd moved to L.A. to become a movie star.

Pretty soon—two, three years, tops—she'd be rich and popular again. And then everything would be easy, the way it used to be.

She knocked. A man in his twenties with a long face and bristly black hair answered the door. He was wearing jeans and a Metallica T-shirt.

"Hello," Cordelia said brightly. "I'm from Wolfram and Hart. Is Sarah Clark in?"

"Uh, no, she isn't here," the man said.

"And you are . . . ?"

"I'm her roommate, Bill. Look, she's kind of— missing, right now. But I'm sure she's gonna pay her bill."

"That's . . . what I wanted to talk to you about," Cordelia said. "Can I come in?"

"Well . . . okay."

Just think Ally McBeal and you'll be fine, Cordelia thought to herself as she strode inside. *Damn. I should have worn a shorter skirt.*

"Now then, Mr. . . . Bill," Cordelia said, consulting her clipboard. "Are you familiar with Ms. Clark's case?"

"Well, I know you helped her out on those drug-smuggling charges, and she was really grateful. But when you never sent her a bill . . ."

"You thought we'd just forget about it. Well, Wolfram and Hart is *not* that kind of firm, mister. We're used to dealing with some very bad customers, and when one of our customers is bad, we take it very—badly."

Bill looked a little confused. "Customers? Don't you mean clients?"

Cordelia sighed, and tried to look sorry for Bill and slightly annoyed at the same time. "You've been watching too much TV, Bill. A *client* is someone who pays what she owes. A *customer* is what we call someone who—*you* know."

Bill gulped. "Disappears?"

"She can't hide forever, Bill. Trust me—I know. I'm a *lawyer.*"

She left Bill looking nervous and promising to call if he heard anything. "Detecting," Cordelia said to herself with a smile as she walked away. "Nothing to it. And I am *so* legal . . ."

The lifeguards left shortly after the sun set. Doyle took the man, who resembled a tanned Mr. Clean with a bushy blond mustache, while Angel followed the woman, an equally tanned, tall brunette. Doyle and Angel stayed in touch via cell phone.

"He's goin' into an underground garage with an electric gate," Doyle reported. "I'm gonna try and slip in behind him . . . okay, I did it, but he's givin' me a funny look in his rearview mirror. Prob'ly thinks I'm some kinda lowlife punk."

"Doyle, you're driving a brand new Mercedes."

"Oh. Right. Kinda hard to get used to. Handles like a dream, though . . . okay, he's gettin' out of the car. Headin' for the elevator. He's stopped. Looks a bit confused. Maybe he forgot somethin' in the car—no, he's headin' for the corner. There's somethin' there, looks like some kind of flower growin' out of a crack. He's bendin' over and smellin' it— Wait. I think I hear somethin', a kind of rumble— the wall's cavin' in! *This is it!*"

"Doyle! Try and hold them off! I'll be there as soon as I can—"

Doyle grabbed the tire iron from the floor and jumped out of the car. He ran toward the lifeguard, who seemed oblivious. The wall had crumbled into a tide of gray dust that pooled around the lifeguard's knees; it reached halfway up the white stalk of the strange black and red flower that engrossed him. A hulking figure was outlined in the shadows beyond the hole in the wall.

Doyle reached the lifeguard, grabbed him by the shoulder and whirled him around. "Hey! Pal! We gotta get outta here!"

The man looked dazed. "Coney Island," he said. "Hot dogs. Cotton candy. Jennifer Gianni's shampoo."

"Right, sure. I understand." He grabbed the man's wrist and yanked him in the direction of the Mercedes. The man took a few faltering steps, then stopped and planted his feet. Doyle came to an abrupt halt; the lifeguard was a lot bigger and beefier than he was.

"No, I—I can't leave. It's been so long . . ."

Doyle considered braining him with the tire iron, but then he'd have to carry him. If he didn't kill him, that was.

The strange flower sank into the pile of dust, folding itself up as it went. A second after it disappeared, the shadowy figure stepped forward out of the hole.

"Mother o' God," Doyle breathed. "Well, I guess it's up to me."

He raised the tire iron and stepped between the demon and his victim.

Another Tremblor stepped out of the hole. And a third.

"Like that's gonna make a difference," Doyle muttered to himself. "I was dead meat after the first one. After the first *quarter* of the first one. This just makes me look stupid . . ."

The first Tremblor stepped forward. He pointed at the lifeguard with one clawed hand, the message obvious: *Give him to us*.

"You guys have got it all wrong," Doyle said. "This isn't who you want. Really. That's why I'm here. The boss sent me to straighten y'out before you made a *horrible* mistake."

The Tremblor said nothing, but his rocky brow furrowed. *Wolfram and Hart?* he projected.

Doyle heard the words *Wolfram and Hart* inside his head, but mistook them for a burst of fear-fueled inspiration. "Wolfram and Hart! They told me—*personally*—t'stop this. I mean, t'ask you *politely* to stop this."

We did as you requested. This is One of the Four; he has the (concept) upon him. We will take him now.

Doyle realized the thoughts he was hearing weren't his own. *Sod this*, he thought before he could stop himself.

The lifeguard seemed to be coming out of his daze. "Hey, what's going on here?" he demanded, shaking free of Doyle's grasp.

Doyle jerked a thumb at himself. "*Good* guy," he snapped. He pointed the tire iron at the Tremblors. "*Bad* guys."

The Tremblors attacked.

They moved as one, unified by telepathy. The first Tremblor charged Doyle, while the other two moved to either side, trying to get to the lifeguard.

Doyle swung the tire iron. It connected with the Tremblor's head with a solid *clang!* but didn't slow him down. The Quake demon swatted him aside with one clawed hand; Doyle sailed through the air, stopping when he hit the side of a Volvo. He fell to the ground with the breath knocked out of him.

He staggered to his feet. His right shoulder and arm were completely numb, but he picked up the tire iron with his left. "Okay," he wheezed. "*Now* you're in for it . . ."

The lifeguard had turned to run, but he'd only gotten a few steps away when one of the Tremblors lashed out with his tail, catching him behind the knees and sending him to the concrete. Instead of trying to get to his feet, he rolled under a Cadillac before they could grab him.

Which is when Angel's car crashed through the security gate.

The gate, the kind that lowered from the ceiling like a garage door, caught on the bumper and tore off. The convertible, wearing the gate like some kind of huge metal flyswatter, roared up to the pair of Tremblors and slammed into them, picking them up and carrying them backward until they broadsided a minivan with a crash of rending metal.

Angel leapt out of the driver's seat.

This time, he had a pickax.

The remaining Tremblor was dragging the lifeguard out from beneath the Caddy by one leg. Angel drove the pickax full-force into the back of the demon's head.

It stuck there.

The Tremblor whirled around, tearing the handle from Angel's hands.

You again, the demon thought at him.

"Telepathic, huh?" Angel said. "That's right, me again. And this time you're on my turf."

Your weapon is useless. The Tremblor ignored the pickax completely. He advanced on Angel, his tail thrashing angrily.

"Aaaaaah!" Doyle yelled, and ran at the Tremblor with his tire iron held high. He let his demon half surface as he charged; his complexion darkened to blue-gray and his face transformed, spikes erupting from his skin like fast-growing thorns.

He swung the tire iron as hard as he could, catching the pickax at the juncture of its shaft and its head, and succeeded in driving the point of the pick a few inches deeper into the demon's skull.

The Tremblor paused.

(. . .) he thought. He didn't move.

Angel began to cautiously edge around him. The Tremblor stayed motionless.

"Good job," he told Doyle without taking his eyes off the Tremblor. "I think you stunned him."

"Do you hear that, or is th'noise just inside my head?" Doyle asked groggily. A low rumble shook the air, growing louder every second—and then the gate pinning the two demons to the minivan suddenly exploded outward. A flying chunk of metal clipped

Doyle on the side of the head, and he collapsed without a sound, reverting to human as he did so.

Angel wasn't as lucky; steel bars impaled his neck, torso and one of his legs. The pain was enough to drive him to one knee, but that was fine; as long as he could still feel, his head was still attached, which meant he'd survive. Decapitation wasn't as widely used as a stake through the heart, but it would destroy a vampire just as surely.

The two Tremblors he'd pinned to the minivan were now free. One stalked toward the lifeguard, who was sitting sprawled on the ground. There was a metal bar projecting from just below his collarbone; he was touching it gingerly, his face pale with shock. The Tremblor grabbed him unceremoniously by the arm and began dragging him toward the hole in the wall. Halfway there, the lifeguard passed out.

The other Tremblor approached Angel, who managed to get to his feet.

You fought well.

"I'm not finished."

Yes, you are. Your ally is unconcious. You are badly wounded and weaponless. You cannot hinder us further.

"Fine. Mind if I leave, then?"

You are free to go.

Angel turned and began to limp away.

❖   ❖   ❖

The Tremblor watched him go, then gave the mental equivalent of a shrug. His people were tenacious—warrior-priests especially so—but these Skin-Dwellers seemed like creatures ruled by whim, their motives and reasoning as changeable as mercury. He doubted if this one had the memory, let alone the will, to interfere with their sacred mission again.

He turned to Baasalt to see if he was all right. The strange implement still jutted from the back of Baasalt's head, and Baasalt hadn't moved since he'd been struck the second time.

He reached out with his mind and touched Baasalt's presence gently. *Baasalt? Are you whole?*

(. . . ° . . .)

This was something the Tremblor had never heard before. He didn't know how to respond; it was unprecedented. Tremblors did not deal well with change, and change in themselves was almost inconceivable.

I don't understand, he projected. *Could you repeat that?* He thought he heard a roaring noise, but ignored it—the Skin of the World was a noisy place.

Angel rammed him with the Mercedes.

The car plowed into the demon, knocking him onto the hood. The vehicle continued to accelerate until it rammed headfirst into the far wall.

It did a good job of embedding the Tremblor there.

The airbag inflated on impact, saving Angel from a serious head injury. Unfortunately, it also violently wrenched aside three of the metal bars currently stuck in his body.

This time, the pain made him pass out.

CHAPTER SIX

Baasalt was a creature made of rock. His body reacted to tempered steel the way a biological organism might react to a concentrated stimulant—and when the tip of the pickax penetrated his brain, he had an epiphany.

The walls between memory and thought shattered. Connections sparked throughout his mind. Ideas started to generate spontaneously. His was not a race given much to imagination—but that was exactly what suddenly engulfed his mind.

He was barely aware of the outside world. It didn't seem important anymore.

The rush of imagery and concepts eventually slowed to a manageable pace, and he came back to himself. He looked around with new eyes.

One of the metal bugs had pinned Maarl to the

wall. Feldspaar was standing at the tunnel entrance, the unconscious form of the one they had come for slung over his shoulder. Another unmoving Skin-Dweller lay on the ground a few feet away.

Maarl does not respond, Feldspaar thought at him.

Leave him, Baasalt thought. *The Third of the Four is the important thing. We must go before we attract more attention; the Skin-Dwellers will swarm over this place like metal bugs to an abundant source of energy.*

Feldspaar's thoughts showed the analogy confused him, but he turned and trudged into the tunnel. Baasalt followed him.

He almost forgot to collapse the tunnel behind him to forestall pursuit. He had a lot to think about. . . .

When Angel came to, he was confused. At first he thought someone had wrapped him in a burial shroud, but he was sitting behind the wheel of a car.

Maybe they were going to bury him in the car. Maybe it was a car he really liked.

Then he realized the shroud was just the punctured remains of the airbag. The pieces of metal sticking out of his body had ripped several large gashes in the material.

Through the cracked windshield, he could see a Tremblor right in front of him.

It was the one he'd hit with the Mercedes, and he wasn't moving. Actually, he seemed embedded in the concrete wall—but somehow, Angel doubted he was dead.

He grabbed the bar protruding from his own chest, gritted his teeth and yanked it out. He did the same with the others, as quickly as he could. All this commotion was going to attract attention.

He climbed out through the shattered driver's window and looked around. Doyle was sitting up, rubbing a bloody gash on his head, but the other Tremblors and the lifeguard were gone.

He limped over to Doyle and helped him to his feet. "You okay?"

"Yeah, yeah. Just don't ask me anything hard, like my name."

Angel inspected the front of his convertible. It was bashed in a bit, but the shockwave the Tremblors had generated to destroy the gate didn't seem to have affected it. He started it up, backed away from the minivan and parked next to the crashed Mercedes.

Angel popped open the trunk and got out a crowbar. "Doyle, give me a hand."

"What's up?" Doyle said. He pulled a flask out of his pocket and took a long, deep swig.

"We're taking a little something home with us."

The Tremblor sat slumped in the chair. A heavy towing chain was wrapped around his body, pinning his arms to his sides. The demon hadn't moved for hours, not since they'd pried him from the wall and hauled him across town to the office.

It was morning now. They'd spent the night trying to figure out how to interrogate him.

"Jackhammer?" Doyle suggested.

"Too noisy."

"Dynamite?"

"I'd like to do this *without* destroying the office."

"*Barney* marathon?"

"Without destroying the office *or* my sanity. Anyway, I don't want to torture the thing, just intimidate him into giving us some information."

"Well, we better figure out the intimidating part before he wakes up, 'cause right now *I'm* the one who's scared of *him*."

The door opened and Cordelia strode in. "And she's back—Cordelia PI! Coming soon to Fox—"

She stopped dead as soon as she noticed the Tremblor. "Euuw. Is that a Quake demon? I thought he'd look more—Amish."

"You're thinkin' of Quakers," Doyle said. "The guys that make the oatmeal."

127

"Oatmeal is made by demons? No wonder I prefer croissants. What's he doing here?"

"We're trying to think of a way to make him talk," Angel said.

"Well, first you've got to wake him up," Cordelia said. She grabbed a glass of water sitting on her desk and threw it in the Tremblor's face.

"Cordy, no!" Doyle blurted out.

"Too late," Angel growled.

The demon's eyes opened. The chair he sat on began to shake. The chains binding him vibrated furiously—then links started snapping, one by one.

"Hey!" Cordelia said. "Hey, that's *my chair!*"

"Get down!" Angel shouted.

All three of them hit the floor as the chain exploded, showering the office with shrapnel. The Tremblor lurched to his feet.

"Great," Angel said under his breath. "And I'm *out* of pickaxes."

He jumped to his feet and faced off against the demon. "Surrender," Angel said. "Or be destroyed."

Never!

He swung at Angel and the vampire dodged back, out of the demon's reach. The Tremblor's tail thrashed, knocking over the table with the coffeemaker on it.

"Get him!" Cordelia demanded.

"Weapons!" Doyle said, and dashed into Angel's

office. He reached for the first big, sharp thing he saw, a broadsword hanging on the wall. It was almost as long as Doyle was tall; he grabbed it with both hands, slung it over his shoulder and rushed back into the fray.

Angel was doing his best to stay out of reach of the demon's hands, while Cordelia confused the Tremblor by throwing whatever she could lay her hands on. Doyle stopped, braced himself and yelled, "Back off, y'rocky bugger! This is a *magic* sword!"

The Tremblor hesitated.

"It is?" Cordelia said. Angel shot her a warning glance.

"What's the matter, you never heard of the—the sword in the stone? Why, this blade has hacked up more boulders than, than . . ."

"Than any *other* sword in the stone," Angel said.

The Tremblor glared at them suspiciously. *I have heard tales of such a sword* . . . he thought at them.

"Angel, Doyle!" Cordelia snapped. "Get over here, quick!" She threw open the window.

Angel and Doyle exchanged glances. Angel nodded, almost imperceptibly, and they both charged the demon.

Angel hit him high, with a flying kick. Doyle thrust for the demon's guts with the point of the sword, as hard as he could. Neither blow did any appreciable damage . . . but they did succeed in knocking him off-balance. He fell backward, stumbled, and crashed halfway through the window before grabbing hold of the sill.

And screamed.

"NOOO! NOOOO! The Void! THE VOID!"

He was staring straight up into the smoggy sky. "Too big, too big," he whimpered. He sounded like he was in shock.

They pulled him back inside, Angel carefully avoiding the sunlight, and the Tremblor collapsed on the floor in a shaking heap. He suddenly seemed about as dangerous as a frightened puppy.

"O' course," Doyle exclaimed. "He's spent his whole life underground—he's agoraphobic!"

"He's afraid of sweaters?" Cordelia said.

"No," said Angel. "He's afraid of wide-open spaces. Good thinking, Cordelia."

"Actually, I just wanted you to throw him out the window," Cordelia replied. "I mean, *look* at this mess. Can't you fight outside for a change?"

Have you ever wondered why we don't do anything? Baasalt thought.

No, I haven't, Feldspaar thought back. He and Baasalt were returning home with their captive. They had been trudging along for some time, descending deeper and deeper into the earth.

Feldspaar had been thinking about Maarl; death was a rare thing among their kind, and he couldn't bring himself to really believe Maarl could be gone. It was just too big a change.

We live, Baasalt continued, *but we don't affect the world around us. We warrior-priests have our holy duties, but most Tremblors spend their lives merely existing. Don't you think?*

I think you should take that thing out of your head, Feldspaar replied. *It doesn't belong there.*

Baasalt had refused to remove the pickax from his skull, insisting it was causing him no harm. *It's some sort of magical artifact*, he declared. *I see everything as if for the first time.*

Your thoughts are strange. They do not flow in an orderly way.

They do not flow—they gush! Baasalt stopped and threw his arms open wide. *Oh, I wish I could properly convey the impressions dancing in my brain!*

Feldspaar didn't know *what* to think about that.

"Talk," Angel said. "Or I'll open the box again."

They were on the roof of their building. Doyle and Cordelia had rigged up a sun-shelter out of blankets for their boss, and a large crate scavenged from the alley made an impromptu cage for their prisoner. Angel sat in a lawn chair underneath his makeshift tent holding a string; the other end was attached to a piece of cardboard serving as the crate's lid.

No! I will not betray my people!

Angel pulled on the string. A crack of daylight appeared between the top of the crate and the lid.

Aaah! No, no, not the Void! I'll tell you what I know!

Doyle and Cordelia stood a little way off, Doyle leaning on a ventilator hood and Cordelia with her arms crossed. "It's kind of creepy," Cordelia said. "The way it talks without talking? Right into your *head*. It can't do some kind of mental whammy, can it?"

"I don't think we have to worry about his brain power," Doyle said. "So far, he hasn't even figured out he can just close his eyes."

"Tell me about the fourth victim," Angel said. "Who is it?"

I do not know the Skin-Dweller's name.

"But you know where to find him."

Baasalt knows. His tuber has the scent of the marked places.

"Baasalt. Is that your leader?"

He is First Warrior-Priest. It is his duty to find the Four.

"You said there were 'marked places.' How are they marked?"

They are marked by our allies on the Skin of the World. It makes it easier to find the Four.

Angel leaned forward in his lawn chair. "Who are your allies on the Skin of the World?"

They are Skin-Dwellers, like you. They speak only to Baasalt.

"Do they have a name?"

I do not know.

Angel yanked on the string, letting the top flap open for just a second. The Tremblor's horrified mental scream made both Cordelia and Doyle grab their heads.

"Tell me their name! Is it the Serpentene? Wolfram and Hart? *Tell me!*"

Please let me go, oh please let me go home . . .

There was a slight breeze on the rooftop, and it shifted just then. Suddenly, Angel was sure he could smell lemon trees, and just the faintest trace of burning wood.

Baasalt and Feldspaar stood before the Grounding, the ruling council of the Tremblors. There were six members, and they stood in a semicircle in a cave miles below the surface. They resembled stone columns that reached from the floor of the cave to the ceiling, for they were one with the rock surrounding them.

The warrior-priests had delivered their hostage, and now Baasalt was making his report.

The Skin of the World is a chaotic, disorganized place, Baasalt thought. *We accepted the help of the Skin-Dwellers for just this reason; they can navigate the shifting currents of their culture to provide us with what we seek, within the Skin-Dweller's time span instead of our own. But there is another way, a way to impose the order of our society on the unpredictability of theirs.*

Go on.

We must dominate the Skin of the World.

Impossible! It is a seething river of madness!

Then we must dam that river. We must change the Skin of the World into a place of restraint and control. Baasalt began to pace in front of the council, a severe breach of etiquette. The pick in the back of his head bobbed up and down as he nodded to himself. *And we can do this, Great Batholith—it is within our power.*

To do what? Lay waste to the Skin of the World? Where then would we find sacrifices for the Crushing of Souls?

It is not the Skin of the World I suggest we attack. It is the Void itself.

The Grounding gave the telepathic equivalent of a collective gasp. *Unthinkable!*

Nothing is unthinkable. I understand that now . . . listen to me. There are places where Blood from the Heart of the World flows onto the Skin. Sometimes, it

134

explodes upward with great fury—and the Void is filled with minute bits of the Blood of the World.

This we know. The Void transforms them and they settle, to become one with the Body of the World again.

But is it only the Blood which is transformed? Is not the Void itself changed by having the Blood within it?

These are questions with no answers.

But the answers can be found, if only the questions are asked. And here is the question which I ask of you, the question which must be asked. What would occur if the Blood at the Heart of the World was unleashed upon the Skin—not at one or five or a dozen spots, but hundreds, thousands of places simultaneously? Unleashed with the full force and majesty it is capable of? What would happen then, esteemed council members?

The Grounding was silent once more. It was hours before they communicated again, the equivalent of a lengthy pause. Finally, their leader, the Batholith, broadcast his response.

The Void, terrible though it is, cannot be mightier than the Heart of the World. Should we unleash its full power, the Void would be filled.

The Void filled. It was a concept no Tremblor had ever even considered, at the same time both exhilarating and blasphemous.

We need to think on this. Go and fulfill your mission. Bring the Fourth to us—and we will discuss this idea further.

As you wish.

Doyle and Cordelia waited downstairs in the office.

"It's not like he's actually *torturing* him," Cordelia said.

" 'Course not."

"And we *are* trying to stop something terrible from happening."

"That we are."

Cordelia picked up some papers from her desk and opened a file cabinet. "And it's not like we could just *ask*. 'Excuse me, Mr. Demon? I understand that you're trying to wreck the city and all, and I was just wondering if you could share a few of the details with us.' Like *that* would work."

Doyle poured himself a cup of coffee. "Highly unlikely."

Cordelia started cramming papers into file folders. "So it's not like Angel has a choice. And hey, it's not like he hasn't done this kind of thing before, right? I mean, this way at least his hundred years of torturing experience aren't going to waste."

"Hard t'argue with that."

Cordelia whirled around and glared at Doyle.

"Will you *please* stop agreeing with me? I feel bad enough as it is."

Doyle put up his hands in surrender. "Take it easy. I know this is hard to justify—though you were doin' a bang-up job, I gotta say—but it *is* necessary. Angel won't actually hurt him, just scare him a little."

Cordelia sighed and collapsed into a chair. "I know, I know. I just hate feeling guilty, okay? I'm not *used* to it."

"Just remember, we're on the side of the angels."

"Please, Doyle. Bad puns are not the way to cheer me up."

"Well, I don't know if there's such a thing as a *good* pun . . ."

Angel came in. "I think I've gotten all the information out of him I can."

"Is he—" Cordelia began.

"What?"

"Still in one piece?"

"Not really. He sort of shattered, actually."

"Shattered?" Cordelia said.

"When he hit the ground. After I threw him off the roof."

"Angel, that was *not* called for," Cordelia snapped. "I mean, *sure* he was a hideous demon, and *sure,* he would have killed you given the chance—okay, he probably would have killed *all* of us. Actually, killing everyone in the city seemed to be on his to-do list. Never mind."

"Relax," Angel said. "I was kidding. He's still cowering in his box."

"So what did you find out?" Doyle asked.

"Possibly the location of the next target. And get this—even though they're still missing someone close to earth, they aren't going after a Serpentene victim."

"Why not?" asked Cordelia.

"He didn't know, but as far as the Serpentene goes, the Tremblors don't seem to bear them any personal ill will. Apparently the only reason the Serpentene's home was attacked was because the Tremblor's mysterious allies asked them to.

"What he does know is that earth is the element most vital to the ceremony, and has to be chosen with care. He knew which direction they were headed in next, and when the snatch was going to take place. He gave me a mental picture of around how far away it was." Angel motioned them to follow him into his office, where the map was still spread out on the floor. "And that would put the location of the next kidnapping around . . . here."

"I know that area," Doyle said. "There's a big graveyard, right there." He tapped the map with one finger.

"A graveyard. Makes sense," Angel admitted. "I

just wish I knew why they'd given up on the Serpentene, especially after they'd returned to trash the place. Something isn't right."

"So, I guess we're stakin' the place out?" Doyle asked.

Angel nodded.

Doyle stretched and yawned. "Better get some shut-eye then, don't you think? Must be close to bedtime for the dentally-enhanced."

"Good idea."

"All right, then. 'Night, boss." Doyle waved good-bye to Cordelia and headed for the door.

After Doyle had left, Cordelia asked, "Is it hard? The torture, I mean."

"It's—emotionally draining."

"Is that because you find it difficult to hurt another living being, or just that you're out of practice?"

"Actually, you'd be surprised how easily it all comes back. Like riding a bike, I guess."

"Or dragging someone behind one . . . did you find anything else out?"

"Like what?"

"I don't know—like his *name?*"

"Rule of torture number one: never personalize your victim. If you start thinking of them as a person, you can't be objective about what you need to do."

Cordelia looked at Angel and arched her eyebrows. She waited.

Angel sighed. "His name is Maarl."

"I *knew* you couldn't pass up a chance to grab some high-quality angst. That's like me saying no to a shoe sale."

Angel sat down behind his desk. "Well, I never was much good at the objective part. The victim's name was usually the *first* thing I got—made the whole process more intimate."

"Okay, that's the kind of statement that makes me sorry we're on a first-name basis. And people say they're amazed at the things that come out of *my* mouth."

"Anyway, I wasn't going for more angst—I was trying to get inside his head. Get a feel for what the Tremblors are like, for who they are and what they want."

"How very Hannibal Lecter of you." Cordelia frowned. "But don't we already *know* what they want?"

"We know what they're after, but we didn't know why. Now I do."

Cordelia picked up a stack of books on Angel's desk and started reshelving them. "Is this something I want to know, or will I sleep better in blissful ignorance?"

"It's how they reproduce."

"There's a joke there that's *so* obvious I'm glad Doyle's gone home."

"Uh—right. Anyway, the Crushing of Souls ritual doesn't just cause an earthquake; it collects all the souls of the people who are killed by the quake. Then it basically . . . *compresses* them. It takes a thousand human souls to make one new Tremblor, apparently because their bodies are so dense."

"Tell me about it. My chair is toast." Cordelia put the last book on the shelf and straightened a mace that was hung next to the door. "So instead of sex, they have to kill a bunch of people and use this ritual to squish their souls into a new demon. Sounds like the Play-Doh factory I used to have."

"Sounds like my sex life . . ."

Cordelia laughed, then covered her mouth. "Sorry. I keep forgetting you actually have a sense of humor."

"It's a common mistake."

"So what do these demons *do* when they're not running around kidnapping people?"

"They think, mainly."

"About what? Different squishing techniques?"

"Theoretical mathematics, a lot of the time. They design and play telepathic games that make three-dimensional chess look like tic-tac-toe. They meditate."

"So they're like—geeks."

"Excuse me?"

"You know, a geek. Anybody in high school who spent all their time doing math, playing chess, and was incapable of having sex."

"Outsiders." Angel nodded.

"Oh, don't try to make them sound all romantic. They were *losers*. I should know." Cordelia sat down across from Angel.

"Because you were a winner?"

"That goes without saying. But I *dated* a loser."

"Xander."

"Yes, and please don't say that name without spitting. *Can* vampires spit? Anyway, if even a loser like him could find people to hang out with, it goes to show that there are no such things as outsiders— just a bunch of little groups of insiders. Some groups just dress better than others."

"That's one way of looking at it. As long as there are others like you around."

"Well, there was nobody *really* like me, so it was a bit of a struggle. But I managed."

Angel looked at her, but didn't say anything.

Cordelia frowned. "What? Oh, you're talking about *you*. Well, what I said still applies; there's nobody really like *you*, either."

"Thanks. That's very reassuring."

"There's nobody really like *anybody*, Angel. Everybody's different."

"So everybody's alone?"

Cordelia rolled her eyes. "You know, you're like a walking advertisment for Prozac. My point is, people don't hang together because they're all exactly the same."

Angel looked thoughtful. "I guess not. They come together because they have common interests, or common enemies, or even for financial reasons."

"Um—sure. And because being alone sucks."

Angel winced. "Doyle isn't the only one making bad puns."

"Sorry. Anyway, shouldn't you be getting some Z's?"

"You're right. I'll see you in a few hours." Angel got up and headed to the freight elevator at the back of his office. He closed the folding metal gate, hesitated, then said, "Cordelia?"

Cordelia paused in the doorway between the inner and outer offices and turned around. "Yes?"

"What *was* the joke that was too . . . *obvious* to make?"

Cordelia grinned. "Angel, please. When the Tremblors reproduce . . ."

"What?"

"The earth moves . . ."

I don't believe this is a good idea, Feldspaar thought.

I have a theory I wish to test, Baasalt replied. *It won't take long.*

It was during the period the Skin-Dwellers called "day," when the burning orb that lived in the Void permeated everything with light; it was a condition Feldspaar found unnatural and frightening. They were inside a structure that also filled him with dread; it had a transparent roof and walls, which protected them from the Void but left them exposed to it at the same time. The shade of the plants that the structure was filled with helped somewhat, but even the plants were deformed and surreal; instead of the twisting, gnarly shapes of proper plants that grew into the earth, these were tall and straight and had bright green parts that twitched if you so much as brushed against them.

They were crouched at the end of a long row of these plants, Feldspaar trying not to look up. Baasalt had a small pile of granite chunks at his feet; each was almost too big for his claws to close around.

What are we waiting for? Feldspaar thought.

That. Baasalt pointed.

At the end of the row a Skin-Dweller had appeared. It was at least a hundred feet away, and busy doing something to the plants; it hadn't noticed them.

Baasalt picked up one of the granite chunks and hefted it. He drew his arm back—and did something Feldspaar had never seen before.

Baasalt snapped his arm forward, and let go of the rock. It *flew*.

Its flight was halted abruptly when it struck a plant close to the Skin-Dweller. The Dweller looked their way, surprised. It began to walk toward them.

"Hey! What are you doing in here—"

Baasalt selected another rock and repeated the action. Again, Feldspaar was astonished when the piece of granite sailed through the Void; it seemed impossible, a violation of everything he believed in.

This time, the rock struck the Skin-Dweller in the face. There was a wet, scarlet explosion, and the figure crumpled to the floor.

Feldspaar looked to his superior and got an even bigger shock.

Baasalt was looking *up*. Up through the transparent roof, up into the Void itself. Feldspaar got a brief glimpse of a hideous, unnatural blue before he slammed his eyes shut—but he could still taste the flavor of Baasalt's thoughts. They were not full of terror, as he would have expected, but instead radiated an intense exhilaration. It was too much for Feldspaar; he turned his own mind away from Baasalt's, though he could still feel the burning of his feelings like the heat from a pool of molten rock.

A full minute passed.

At last, the intensity of Baasalt's thoughts faded.

Baasalt? Feldspaar asked. *Are you . . . all right?*

I am glorious. And most importantly—I am no longer afraid.

CHAPTER SEVEN

Doyle had been completely serious about blowing his money at the track. He'd come dangerously close to actually winning at one point, but fortunately that had proved to be a false alarm.

Now he was down to his last few dollars, and he was about to dispose of them by ordering a drink. He could have gotten rid of them just as effectively by buying something frivolous—like food—but Doyle firmly believed that once you committed to a plan, you stuck to it. Down-and-out was what he was aiming for, and spending the last of his cash on booze seemed the way to go.

And then there was the other thing—the thing he *hadn't* told Angel about.

Hell, Doyle thought. *If this doesn't work, I'll see what I can do about goin' into debt. Goin' deeper into debt, anyway.*

147

The bar he'd picked to spend his last few dollars in was not the kind of place to let him run a tab; it made the dive he'd taken Angel to look like the lounge at the Four Seasons. The only season this place was familiar with was Happy Hour, which lasted from seven A.M until closing and wasn't particularly happy. Doyle supposed that Surly All Day Long just didn't have the right ring to it.

The place didn't even have a proper bar, just an oversized counter in one corner with a bearded giant pouring drinks behind it. It wouldn't have surprised Doyle if he'd been told that the real bartender was lying in a pool of blood behind the bar, and the gentleman drawing a pitcher of beer was actually a psychotic biker with a dry throat and a bad temper.

Not to mention a face covered with the worst tattoos Doyle had ever seen. Either that, or the most artistic birthmarks.

There weren't any booths either, just tables scattered around a small room with chairs that didn't match. A roach scuttled across his table, made it halfway, and got beaten up by another roach. It was that kind of bar.

The second the whiskey touched his lips, he heard Graedeker's voice.

"Now, what do you think *his* story is?" Graedeker

asked. He sat down at Doyle's table without waiting for an invitation. Doyle hadn't heard him walk up, but Graedeker was always doing stuff like that. He liked to play the man of mystery.

Graedeker himself looked about as mysterious as a shoe salesman. He had a wide, friendly face, balding on top and jowly at the bottom, with sunken brown eyes and a bulbous nose. He was paunchy but not fat, of average height, and had shoulders that slumped. He was dressed in a cheap beige suit, without a tie.

"Graedeker," Doyle said with a smile. "Who's story are we talkin' about?"

"The bartender," Graedeker said. "Those tattoos—Good God, eh? Never seen the like."

"Here's my theory," Doyle said. "He's a tattoo artist himself, right? Comes home to his old lady after a weekend of hard partyin' with the biker gang he runs with, demands sex, throws up on her halfway through and passes out. Well, she's had enough. So she gets his electric needle and some ink, and starts to express her opinion of him on his face—but she loses her nerve when she realizes what he'll do to her when he wakes up. Right about then their five-year-old daughter comes in and says *she* wants to draw on Daddy, too. His old lady grins, hands over the electric needle and tells her kid to go to it."

The bar had a waitress, a young woman who might have been attractive; it was hard to tell under the multiple piercings and heavy makeup. She came over to the table and Graedeker ordered a beer from her. She managed the whole transaction, payment to delivery, without saying a word.

"What about her?" Graedeker asked.

"Deaf mute with a chrome fetish. Goes to thrash concerts just to feel all that metal vibratin' in her head."

Graedeker chuckled. "Ah, Doyle. I like to watch people, but I could never come up with stories like those."

"Well, we all have our talents, right? Yours seem a touch more profitable than mine."

"I take it your finances are somewhat unstable?"

"My finances are dead stable. Emphasis on the dead."

"I see. Well, maybe I could help you out."

"I was hopin' you'd say that."

Graedeker took a long swig of beer. "You have something to put up as collateral?"

"As a matter of fact, I do." Doyle reached into his pocket and pulled out an amulet on a silver chain. The amulet was shaped like an eye, with a deep purple gem for the iris. He slid it across the table to Graedeker.

"Hmmm," Graedeker said, picking up the amulet

and studying it. "The Gaze of Tuskara. Where'd you come by this?"

"From my boss. He used it to send a demon back to its own dimension, so I figure it has to be pretty valuable."

"Uh-huh. Well, let's say I'm interested. What sort of loan do you want?"

"It's not exactly a loan I'm interested in. Actually, what I need is some information."

Graedeker's eyes narrowed. He took another sip of beer before he answered. "I guarantee my customers' privacy."

"It's not your customers I'm interested in—more like your competition."

"And who would that be?"

"The Serpentene."

Graedeker frowned. He hefted the amulet in his hand, then glanced around. "I think perhaps we should talk in a more private place. My shop's right around the corner."

"Fine by me."

Graedeker's rig was parked about a block away, in a vacant lot full of weeds and rusting junk. The semitrailer was painted a flat white, the Freightliner rig in front of it a dark brown. It was as unremarkable as Graedeker himself.

Graedeker walked around the back and rapped on the rear door. Bolts slid aside and the door swung open.

The demon on the other side was a little more impressive.

He was big, six and a half feet or so, with scaly white skin like an albino alligator. His skull was too thick and wide at the top; it looked like his brains were about to bulge out of his head. He had huge black eyes, and a thick-lipped mouth full of sharp, crooked teeth. He wore tattered jeans, army boots and a black muscle shirt. Behind him was a black velvet curtain that concealed the rest of the interior.

"This is Leo," Graedeker said. Leo put out a massive, moon-white hand and helped Graedeker into the trailer. Doyle scrambled up after him before Leo offered to help him, too. "Leo's my driver. He also keeps an eye on the shop when I'm not around."

Leo nodded. Doyle nodded back. Leo crossed his arms and did his impression of a statue. Doyle resisted the urge to applaud.

Graedeker drew aside the velvet curtain and motioned Doyle in. "Welcome," he said, "to the Devil's Tulips."

You'd never know you were in the back of an eighteen-wheel truck, Doyle thought. It looked exactly like a little curio shop: a row of glass-paneled display cases formed a counter on one side, while tables and stands were scattered throughout the rest of the floor space, covered with various types of merchandise: African masks, shrunken heads, *non*-shrunken heads, jewelry, weapons, carvings, books, jars with vaguely obscene things floating in them.

The walls were paneled in wood, and light came from a large window set into one wall. Doyle hadn't noticed the window when approaching the truck, and wondered how he could have missed it.

Then he realized what lay on the other side.

It was a scene straight out of Dickens. Snow fell softly while people in Victorian garb strolled past, down what was obviously a street in London. Some of them peered through the window curiously, shading their eyes as if the interior were too dim to make out.

"Neat trick," Doyle said. "How d'you manage it?"

Graedeker was busying himself behind the counter. "Oh, it's a scrying glass I picked up from an Ulgar demon. It relays scenes from wherever the glass happened to be a hundred years ago. Not much practical value, but pretty all the same."

Doyle picked up a voodoo doll and studied it. "Well, you've got somethin' for everybody, don't you?"

"My stock depends on what's available. The Serpentene, though . . . *they've* got something for everyone."

"Then you *do* know about them."

"Oh, yes. And I'll even tell you what I know—but

since this isn't the kind of transaction I usually make, the trade will have to be permanent. I get to keep the Gaze of Tuskara."

"'Uh—okay. It's a deal." *And hopefully Angel will think it's a fair swap.*

Graedeker opened a drawer behind the counter and dropped the amulet inside. He closed the drawer again, locked it, and looked at Doyle. He smiled.

"The Serpentene. Where to begin . . . well, what do you know about them so far?"

"Not much. They're originally from Ireland, they're descended from snakes, and they seem to be as good at spendin' money as they are at makin' it. They keep to themselves, and sunshine puts 'em to sleep. That's about it." He thought for a second. "And they have excellent taste in Scotch."

"Congratulations. That's more than some people ever find out, even after dealing with them for years." Graedeker rummaged around in a cabinet and brought out a bottle and a shot glass. "Speaking of Scotch—care to try a little of this?"

Doyle took the bottle and examined it. "Glen Culkhain? Don't think I've heard of it." The bottle was dusty, made of clear glass with a label that showed a dragon wrapped around an enormous pair of armored legs, with a tiny village in flames between the feet.

"I'd be amazed if you had. It's from a parallel dimension." Graedeker took the bottle back, uncorked it and poured a few drops into the glass. "Distilled by giants, as a matter of fact."

Doyle tasted it carefully. "Very nice," he said.

"It should be. It's over a thousand years old."

Doyle eyed his glass in disbelief. "You treat all your customers this way? Because if you do, I'm sure I can find somethin' else to hock."

Graedeker smiled and shook his head. "Just making a point. I obtained this bottle from someone who had dealings with the Serpentene; I think telling you *his* story is perhaps the best way to tell you about *them*."

"I'm all ears. And tastebuds."

"His name was Rudolpho Faranetti, known to his friends as Icepick Rudy. Rudy was a member of a New York crime family called the Corzatos, and he performed certain unpleasant but necessary jobs for them. This made him both an asset and a liability to the Corzatos, because while Rudy was very good at disposing of problems, he also knew where all those problems were buried, and who ordered them buried in the first place. So even though the Corzatos made sure he was well-rewarded, Rudy was aware that at the slightest sign of betrayal he would disappear, and someone else would take over his job.

"Needless to say, this put Rudy under a lot of pressure. As a lot of people under pressure do, he found a hobby to distract himself. Some men turn to women, some to gambling, some to food; Rudy turned to Scotch.

"Not just any Scotch, though. Rudy become a connoisseur of the finest single malts illicit money could buy. Not only did the drink lessen the tension of his existence, but searching for and sampling the very best bottlings kept him occupied.

"One day he heard an apocryphal story concerning a Scotch called Glen Culkhain. It was said to be made by a race of giants, distilled from tears of happiness and barley grown on the graves of virgins. It was said to be the rarest whiskey in existence, as well as the most expensive—and it produced a most unusual effect in those who drank it. When Rudy heard about this effect, he put the word out: he was looking for such a whiskey, he was willing to pay what it was worth, and he would personally torture to death anyone stupid enough to try to pass off a fake.

"Eventually, he was contacted by one of the Serpentene. They had such a bottle, and they were willing to sell. Would Mr. Faranetti care to sample the product to ensure its authenticity?

"Rudy said he would be delighted.

"They met in a hotel room, as is often the case in

these sorts of deals. Rudy was shown the bottle, and allowed to pour his own shot. Before he sampled it, he told the Serpentene representative—a beautiful young woman—that he had heard a story about the whiskey, that it produced a certain intriguing effect. He asked if the story about this effect were true, and the young woman told him that it was.

"Rudy nodded, and took a sip.

"Rudy had done a lot of bad things in his time. For the most part, those things hadn't bothered him; they were simply how he earned his living. But there was this one job that had been harder than the rest. A lot harder.

"Usually, Rudy didn't know the people he . . . took care of. Occasionally he was asked to extend this service to a colleague, but these instances were rare. In this one particular case, though, he was asked to take care of someone he had known for over twenty years, someone whom he'd grown up with and in fact was very close to. Though it caused him a great deal of sorrow, he chose to accept the job rather than have it performed by a stranger.

"He had carried a heavy burden of guilt and remorse ever since that day . . . until he took that first drink of Glen Culkhain."

Doyle stopped with his own lips an inch from his glass. He met Graedeker's eyes over the rim. "And then what?"

157

"The guilt vanished. That's what this whiskey does. If you take a swallow while holding in your mind that one image from your past that causes you the most regret, it will cease to bother you. It will grant you peace. It will *forgive* you."

"Really? Hang on a second." Doyle's brow furrowed in thought, then he brightened. "Ah." He tossed back the rest of his glass, closed his eyes, and sighed.

"Ah, Bridget," he said softly. "Whenever I see a parole officer, I still think of you . . ."

Doyle set his glass down on the counter. "Bottled absolution. How long does it last?"

"As long as whiskey ever does."

"And what did Rudy pay for this miracle?"

"That I can't tell you, because I don't know. I can, however, tell you what I paid for it: three-quarters of a million dollars."

"And why did Rudy sell it to you?"

"He ran into trouble of a more pragmatic nature, and needed to get out of the country fast. I understand he's no longer employed by the Corzato family."

Graedeker drained his own glass, and returned the bottle to the cabinet. He picked up a jeweler's loupe and fitted it to his eye, then began to examine a ring lying in a small tray. Doyle couldn't help but notice the ring was still around a finger.

"So," Doyle said, "the Serpentene can get hold of some pretty esoteric merchandise. Considerin' their tastes, that's hardly surprisin'."

"It's not just that they can get such merchandise—it's the people they sell it to. Politicians, celebrities, CEOs. They move in some very powerful circles."

"Yeah? They make any powerful enemies?"

"As a matter of fact, I understand there was some unpleasantness recently over a real estate deal. Seems the Serpentene refused a very lucrative offer for some land."

"Oh? I don't suppose you'd happen t'know who made the offer?"

"Of course. It was a law firm—Wolfram and Hart."

"Look," Cordelia said, "I don't care what you do to me. I won't betray the people I work for."

The handsome blond man with the scar on his face moved closer, out of the shadows and into the light. "You don't know who you're dealing with."

Cordelia glared at him. "I know plenty. Who do you think I am, some dumb sexetary? I mean, secretary—"

"Cut!"

"Sorry!" Cordelia said. "I'll get it this time, I promise!"

"That's fine, Ms. Chase," the director said. "We'll just splice together a few of your other takes. We have all we need."

"Okay, then. Thanks!" Cordelia said.

"Clear the set, please," a production assistant said. "We've got another audition to do."

"Oh, right," Cordelia said. She hurried over to where Maureen was sitting at the edge of the set.

"You did great," Maureen told her.

"You really think so?" Cordelia asked.

The Serpentene woman rose from her chair and gave Cordelia a big hug, saying, "Of course! Come on—I'll buy you lunch."

They took Maureen's car to Spago, where they got a booth in the corner. Maureen ordered a double espresso through a yawn.

"Hey, your tongue looks normal," Cordelia said.

"That's because I have two of them," Maureen said. "The forked one is underneath. It doesn't show unless I want it to."

"Huh. So, like, does it give you any special demon abilities?"

"Well, it is sensitive to changes in temperature. Some snakes have what is called a pit organ, which does the same thing. It comes in useful, sometimes; I can tell when my espresso is too hot to drink without actually tasting it, or adjust a hot tub to the perfect temperature without getting in."

"Wow. A demonic power that's useful instead of painful or icky. That beats Angel's whole bag of tricks."

Maureen scanned the menu. "I think I'm in the mood for the turkey ravioli . . . what *are* Angel's tricks, anyway?"

"I think I just want a salad—maybe a lobster salad. Angel's what?"

"His tricks. You know, what he can do."

"Oh, the usual vamp stuff. Really strong, can only be killed by direct sunlight or a stake through the heart, that kind of thing."

"Ah." Maureen's espresso arrived. She thanked the waiter with a smile, then flicked the tip of her forked tongue out over the top of the cup. "Still too hot. I just thought that since he's a different sort of vampire, he might have different powers. Different strengths and weaknesses."

"No, he's pretty much the same as a factory model. Doesn't show up in mirrors, can't stand garlic or crosses or holy water, can't enter a house unless he's been invited in first. You know, there's an awful lot of restrictions to being a vampire, considering the few things you get in return. If I were Angel, I'd complain."

"Well, there is the whole eternal youth thing."

"I suppose—hey, don't you have that, too?"

"Sort of. We live a long time, and we know a few

tricks to keep looking young. But once a skin finally wears out, it deteriorates pretty fast."

"So you go wrinkly all at once?"

"More or less. Then we shed the skin and start over."

"You know, if you could teach people how to do that? You'd put every plastic surgeon in this town out of business."

Maureen chuckled. "Well, it's not as glamorous as it sounds. It itches like you wouldn't believe, for one thing. I'm not looking forward to the next time."

The waiter came back and took their orders. Maureen ordered another double espresso.

"So—if you don't mind me asking—how old *are* you?" Cordelia said.

"Seven hundred," Maureen said.

And then burst out laughing at the look on Cordelia's face. "I'm sorry, I couldn't resist. I'm twenty-eight—this is only my second skin. It's about three years old."

"Snake humor. Right," Cordelia said with an embarrassed grin.

"No, just humor," Maureen said. "We're not really that different from you, you know."

"No, you're not—except *you* know people at Paramount. I can't thank you enough for getting me that audition."

"No problem. When people help us, we help them. . . ."

"This is not helping," Associate Rome said.

He was talking to the man seated on the other side of his desk. The man was small, round, and nervous. His hairless brown head glistened with perspiration, even in the air-conditioned office. He had a habit of rubbing his mustache when he talked that Rome found extremely annoying. His name was Emilio Maldonado.

"Look," Maldonado said. "Seismology isn't an exact science. I can't tell you the exact effects of a large-scale quake, because we haven't *had* a really big one yet. What I *can* do is tell you what we learned from the '94 quake, and make some projections."

Rome stared at Maldonado. He had an imposing stare; deep-set, intense black eyes under a heavy, overhanging brow. It was the only heavy thing about him. The rest was as sharp as the suit he wore: a thin, sharp face, sharp cheekbones, a sharp widow's peak of glossy black hair on a high forehead. A sharp nose and chin above a body as strong and slender as a scimitar. The fingers he steepled together in front of him could have been a concert pianist's.

"I suppose that will have to do," Rome said quietly. His voice rasped like a nail file on prison bars.

There was a large map of the Los Angeles area spread out on the expanse of Rome's desk. Maldonado pointed to the San Fernando Valley with a chubby finger. "On January nineteenth, at 4:31 A.M., there was a seismic event approximately nineteen kilometers below Northridge, around thirty-two kilometers from downtown L.A. It had a moment magnitude of 6.7, as compared to the 6.9 of the one that struck San Franciso in 1989."

Maldonado tapped a spot at the edge of the map. "Now, this was a thrust-fault earthquake. That means that where the tectonic plates meet, one suddenly shifts up and the other shifts down. This type of quake can be the most destructive, generating extremely strong ground motion. The Armenian quake in '88 was a thrust-fault, and it killed 80,000."

"Tell me about property damage."

Maldonado cleared his throat. "Uh, yes, I was getting to that. The Northridge quake, even though it only killed 57 people, was the most expensive disaster in U.S. history—the final toll was in the neighborhood of 40 billion dollars. The severe shaking characteristic of a thrust-fault quake caused massive destruction to the insides of buildings—especially plumbing and gas pipes. Many buildings that survived structurally intact were still rendered unusable by internal damage."

"You don't have to break someone's back to incapacitate them," Rome said. "Soft tissues are much more vulnerable."

"Yes, I—I see the analogy," Maldonado managed. "Uh—" he consulted his notes. "Of the 66,546 buildings inspected afterward, 6 percent were severely damaged, and 17 percent moderately damaged. There was, of course, major damage to many roads and freeways as well. I suppose you could view that as injuries to arteries and veins." He gave Rome a quick, nervous smile.

"I suppose you could."

"Now, despite all this, we were extremely lucky. It was early in the morning on a holiday, so most of the big concrete structures that collapsed—like parking garages—were empty. The death toll could have been in the hundreds, easily."

Rome smiled at that, but said nothing. The smile made Maldonado feel more nervous, not less.

"Unfortunately, this quake did little to relieve the seismic pressure that's been building up for the last hundred years. Chances are good that a major shaker will strike in the next three decades—one that'll make this look like a child's tantrum."

"Details."

"A quake of at least an 8 magnitude is likely. That's the same strength as the one that hit San Francisco in 1906. Chances of such an occurrence are in the—"

"I don't care about probabilities. I need to know about effects."

"Effects, yes. Well, most of the damage in a large quake—especially in a coastal city—can happen indirectly.

"Let's start with broken gas mains. Fires begin to rage. They can't be reported because the alarm system works on underground conduits that have ruptured. The electrical grid is down, and so are the phones. Fire trucks can't get to the fires anyway, because the roads are blocked with rubble and shattered glass. If one does get through, they'll find there's no water—the pipes will have broken. But the fires aren't a problem for too long, because the flooding from the dams that have given way will put them out. It's even conceivable that there could be a tsunami, though that would indicate an offshore epicenter.

"As far as individual structures go, there are three significant failures we can predict. The first is concrete frame buildings: older government buildings, multi-story parking garages. The second is 'soft-story' buildings, apartment buildings constructed primarily from wood—especially the kind built on pillars to accommodate parking on the bottom floor.

"Steel-frame buildings would fare the best—at least, that's what people used to think. Tests done on steel-frame high-rises that survived the Northridge quake were found to have cracks in their welds. These buildings will almost certainly fail, and probably be the most costly."

"Do you have a list of such buildings?"

"Uh . . . yes. Right here." Maldonado fumbled through his briefcase and pulled out a report. Rome took it and began to read it.

Maldonado waited.

"You can go now," Rome said. He didn't look up.

Maldonado left.

What are we going to do now? Feldspaar thought. He desperately wanted an answer, *any* answer. He felt as if all stability had fled from his existence.

The answer he got didn't make him feel any better.

We are going to do more research, Baasalt replied.

Research? I don't understand. Did you not already discover that . . . that which you needed to know? Feldspaar couldn't bring himself to actually mention the stone-hurtling-through-Void incident; he'd rather never think of it again.

They were in a sewer tunnel beneath the city. Baasalt had destroyed some of the cables that ran along the top of the tunnel; he'd told Feldspaar that the Skin-Dwellers would send someone to repair it.

Feldspaar didn't know how the Skin-Dwellers would do this, or how they would even know about the damage.

Baasalt's explanation had made him dizzy; it had to do with the world of the Skin-Dwellers being interconnected in a huge variety of ways, something Baasalt extrapolated from their chaotic and varied nature. Tremblors were connected through mental pathways or tunnels, and that was it.

There are other things I must know, Baasalt thought, *if I am to convince our race of the need for change.*

But the Grounding said they would consider your proposal.

The Grounding will never accept my recommendations. My plans are too radical, too far-reaching. In order to facilitate my ideas, I will have to convince the general population.

And how will you do that? Feldspaar asked weakly.

I will adapt the Skin-Dwellers' methods to my own uses.

A light bobbed toward them out of the darkness, followed by the sound of splashing feet. A Skin-Dweller, the fur-faced kind called a male. Baasalt and Feldspaar were both concealed inside a recess in the tunnel, a recess the Skin-Dweller headed straight for.

When the light fell upon them, Feldspaar froze, blinded. "What the hell—" the Skin-Dweller blurted out, and then Baasalt knocked him down with his tail. The light spun out of his hands and dropped beneath the murky water. It continued to shine, though much more dimly.

Baasalt seized the Skin-Dweller by one wrist and hauled him back to his feet. The male was sputtering and thrashing, but stopped when Baasalt reached out to his mind.

Warrior-priests were trained in making mental contact with other species, but Feldspaar had never seen telepathy used in quite this way before. Baasalt simply forced his way into the male's mind and began to root around.

Feldspaar withdrew his thoughts, shocked. This was like . . . it was like—

That was the problem. It wasn't like anything, at least not anything Feldspaar had experienced. He wished he could just lie down for a few years.

Abruptly, Baasalt withdrew. He released the Skin-Dweller, who slumped down against the tunnel wall in a daze. Baasalt nodded to himself. *Yes, yes, that will do nicely. Just as I suspected.*

He turned suddenly and trudged off down the tunnel. After a moment, Feldspaar followed him.

He wasn't sure why.

❖   ❖   ❖

"This is my daughter Fiona," Maureen said.

"Oh, she's so *sweet,*" Cordelia said. "And she looks so *normal.* Uh—you know what I mean."

The Serpentene child looked at Cordelia doubtfully. She was hardly more than a toddler, with wispy blond hair and big blue eyes. She balanced unsteadily on two chubby legs, clutching the edge of the coffee table for stability.

"You mean she looks human," Maureen said. "But she isn't. For one thing, she spent nine months in an egg instead of in my belly."

"An egg? Hmmm—you know, at first I was going to say 'Euuw,' but actually, that sounds like a lot less trouble than the regular way. The human way, I mean."

"Oh, it is. No morning sickness, no backaches, no mood swings—just make sure the incubator's plugged in."

"Not to mention no maternity clothes or excess cellulite," Cordelia said. "It sounds too good to be true."

"Well, it's not all wine and roses. I still have to balance my job with being a mother, and I can't send her to a regular day-care. Of course, since most of the other Serpentene women are in the same situation, we have a communal day-care center here in the building that the parents take turns overseeing."

"The fathers, too?"

"Oh, yes. Serpentene men are very involved in raising their children."

Cordelia looked around her at the opulent apartment and sighed. "You get all this, babies and responsible dads *too*? Okay—where do I sign up?"

Fiona giggled.

CHAPTER EIGHT

Back at the office, Doyle finished filling in Angel on what he'd learned from Graedeker. "So Wolfram and Hart are definitely involved. The question is, how?"

"Let's run it down," Angel said. He was doing Tai Chi exercises with a sword he held in two hands. He swept the blade slowly through the air. "First, we know that someone asked the Tremblors to attack the Serpentene."

"Check. Second, we know that Wolfram and Hart had a connection to some—maybe all—of the victims."

Angel parried an invisible opponent in slow-motion. "Third, we know someone is feeding information about potential victims to the Tremblors."

Doyle nodded. "Fourth, the obvious conclusion:

Wolfram and Hart are feedin' the Tremblors sacrifices, in return for which they lean on the Serpentene."

Angel brought the sword back to center, then relaxed and dropped the point. "Right. The question is, what are Wolfram and Hart after? If it was just the building, they wouldn't risk destroying it with an earthquake."

"Maybe it's straight blackmail," Doyle suggested. "The Serpentene have a lot of money."

"Maybe. Whatever it is, there's something our employer isn't telling us. I think it's time I had a little talk with Galvin."

"Before or after your dinner with Kate? Speakin' of which, aren't you gonna be late?"

Angel ran for the door, then remembered he had a sword in his hand. He hung the sword on the wall quickly, grabbed his trenchcoat and left.

Baasalt had led Feldspaar back into the depths, but they had not returned to their people—not physically. It was at the midway point between the region the Tremblors called home and the Skin of the World that Baasalt chose to broadcast his message.

People of the Fourth Tribe, hear my thoughts. I, Baasalt, First Warrior-Priest, have knowledge to share with all of you.

His thoughts were forceful, and they echoed throughout the minds of all the Tremblors. Such an announcement was highly unusual; they halted whatever mental gymnastics they were practicing, stopped their calculations, meditations, or communications, and listened.

I have a new game for you.

This was exciting, but hardly unusual; new games were proposed every few centuries. Most were variations of mathematical formulas.

Baasalt called up an image in his mind of a spherical stone. *This is called the ball. The purpose of the game is to intersect a projection of the ball with a shifting complex variable—called a Human—within an established set of parameters, called the Field. The game requires nine players.*

Players position themselves mentally at nine predetermined points on the field. Each has a ball. The complex variable is positioned at the point called Home Plate. The player called the Pitcher projects his ball according to a set of mathematical principles called velocity, inertia and trajectory. The object is to intersect the complex variable in such a way as to reduce its value.

Once the ball is projected, the complex variable begins to shift along a preset path toward the position of First Base. If the ball intersects the complex variable and causes it to collapse, a point is awarded the pitcher and another complex variable is introduced at Home Plate.

If the ball does not intersect the variable, it continues. The player at First Base attempts to intersect the variable with his ball. If the variable reaches First Base without being reduced to zero, it continues toward Second Base, and the player there attempts the same maneuver. This continues until the variable has looped back to Home Plate. The Outfield positions can attempt to intersect the path of the complex variable with a ball at any time.

Positions alternate nine times. At the conclusion, the player with the most points is the winner.

There was a general murmur of interest in the minds of the Tremblor population. More than one wanted to know what the game was called.

It is called Stoning . . .

"Angel? Did you hear what I said?"

Angel looked up. On the other side of the table, Kate was staring at him expectantly.

"Uh—no, I'm sorry. What did you say?"

"I said, how's your soup?"

Angel glanced at his bowl of miso. "It's . . . chunkier than I prefer."

"I can't believe a diet of clear soups keeps you in the shape you're in. Maybe I should try it."

Angel took a sip of sake. "It's a—whole body regimen, actually. You have to avoid a lot of things. It's not for everyone."

"What sorts of things?" Kate picked up a piece of sushi with her chopsticks and dipped it into a mixture of wasabi and soy sauce before popping it into her mouth.

"Oh, certain spices, overexposure to the sun, wood—"

"Wood?"

"Uh—particular types of woods. They can cause an allergic response."

"Oh, I get it. I went to the academy with someone who was allergic to sandalwood. Broke out in hives if she got too close to some kinds of incense."

"Incense is bad. Especially the kind they use in Catholic churches."

"Funny—you don't strike me as the type."

Angel picked up his bowl of soup and sipped from it, Japanese-style. "Well, at least it's salty enough . . . what type is that?"

"The California fad-diet type. I guess I don't really know you that well."

Angel smiled. "I'm more used to asking for information than giving it out."

"Not this time. Unless someone decides to rob this place at gunpoint in the next hour, you're trapped here with me. You're gonna have to make with the small talk, pal."

"Ouch. Are you this rough on all your interrogation subjects?"

Kate grinned, picked up another piece of sushi and and popped it into her mouth. She didn't say a word.

"Okay, I can do small talk . . ." Angel trailed off.

Kate chewed, swallowed. Waited.

"Nice night," Angel said.

"Smog's not too bad," Kate said evenly.

There was a pause.

"How's the sushi?"

"Raw."

"Uh—seen any good movies lately?"

"I rented *The Usual Suspects* the other night. Thought Kevin Spacey was brilliant."

"I—haven't seen it. Actually, I don't go to movies very often."

Kate put down her chopsticks. "Okay, no movie talk. Sports?"

"Never seen the point."

"Books?"

"I read a lot, but it's mostly research, poetry or classics."

"What about current fiction, bestsellers? I like Tom Clancy, myself."

"Does Mark Twain count as current?"

She sighed. "Music?"

Angel brightened. "Absolutely. I love music."

"Now we're getting somewhere. What flavor?"

"I like a lot of the British stuff, actually."

"You mean like Oasis and Blur? Or do you mean older stuff like the Beatles, the Who, the Stones?"

"I was thinking more along the lines of Thomas Augustine Arne or John Field."

Kate frowned. "And those would be?"

"Eighteenth-century composers."

"English ones, of course."

"It's not just the English ones I like. The Germans and the Italians were brilliant, too."

"I see."

"You . . . don't have any idea what I'm talking about, do you?"

"Sorry. My idea of classical music is anything they play on an Oldies station."

"So . . . nice night, isn't it?"

Kate laughed and shook her head.

Thank God for sake, Angel thought, and took another gulp.

They sat in silence for a while, Kate pretending to be absorbed in her tuna roll. Angel wished desperately for something, anything, to say . . . but what did he and Kate have in common, really? He was more than two hundred years her senior, had been born in a century that hadn't seen the invention of the telephone. Her world was based on facts and scientific deduction; his centered around mystic visions and supernatural evil.

He'd gone over to Doyle's place once and found him watching a TV show called *Baywatch*. To Angel, it had seemed to take place on another planet, a planet of shining light and impossibly bright colors. He'd forgotten how sunlight could sparkle on the waves of the ocean. Sometimes, Angel was almost grateful for the guilt he carried. It kept him from thinking about the other, entire world he'd lost.

The world Kate still lived in.

"Tell me about the case you're working on," Kate said. "Did the information I sent over help?"

"It did. Thank you."

"So what exactly is the case? People connected to the four elements—is it some kind of bizarre serial killer thing?"

"Not exactly. I'm hoping the people who disappeared are still alive."

"Got any suspects?"

"Nothing I can talk about, I'm afraid."

"Of course. So . . . nice night."

"Uh—yeah."

Angel signaled the waiter for more sake.

"Cordy! What are you doin' here at this late hour?"

"I'd ask you the same, except I already know: you're sleeping on the couch."

Doyle sat up and stretched sleepily. "Yeah, well, Angel asked me t'stick around and keep an eye on Mr. Flintstone, upstairs. Don't know why; he's practically catatonic."

Cordelia tossed her purse on the desk, then sat on the edge herself. "Doyle, I have had the most amazing day. Maureen got me an audition for a movie! I read for the part of the secretary of the bad guy. I think I really nailed it, too."

"That's great."

Cordelia squinted at him suspiciously. "Doyle, don't 'that's great' me. You show more enthusiasm when you have a dental appointment."

"Cordy, it's not that I'm not happy for you. It's just that—well, I still don't trust the Serpentene. I found out a few things about 'em."

"Like what?"

Doyle got up and walked over to the coffeemaker. He grabbed a cup and then hesitated. There was a mickey of whiskey next to the pot. "Coffee or whiskey?" he muttered. "Ah, the many choices of a rich an' varied life."

He poured himself a cup of coffee, then added a shot of whiskey. "If only they were all this simple—"

"What did you find out about the Serpentene?" Cordelia demanded. "Do they have something contagious, like—like snake cooties? Because I spent all day with Maureen, and we went back to the apartment complex, and I *do* have this funny itchy spot—"

"Nothin' like that. It's just that it seems they deal in more than used cars and real estate." He told her the story about the hitman and the special bottle of Scotch.

"That's it? So they sell people magic stuff. Big deal. Did the Scotch turn him into a—a werescotsman or something?"

"No. But we're talkin' about demons, here, Cordy. They're not known for givin' stuff away. There's always a price."

"I thought you said the price was three-quarters of a million dollars?"

"That's what Graedeker bought it for. He doesn't know what the mob guy paid—and that's the part that worries me."

Cordelia frowned. "Are you saying he traded his soul for a bottle of Scotch? I don't think I believe that—and I work with *you*."

Doyle took a sip from his mug, then nodded. "Doesn't really ring true for me, either. Still, his luck turned bad after he dealt with the Serpentene."

"By *that* standard, you must have hocked your soul a dozen times since I've known you."

"Everythin' but, Cordy. Everythin' but."

Feldspaar was having a crisis of faith.

He was loyal to his tribe and their beliefs. He was

also loyal to the First Warrior-Priest, and sworn to follow his commands without question.

These two things had never come into conflict before.

Baasalt's ideas had stimulated him in a way he had never felt. At first he had found them disturbing, frightening even; but the more he considered them, the more sense they made.

Feldspaar was a warrior-priest—but other than forays for sacrificial victims every few decades, he rarely saw even the chance for battle. His position was more about maintaining the status quo than conquest.

Until now.

Baasalt? he thought. They were back in the sewer tunnels, close to the Skin of the World. *I have some questions.*

Good. Ask them.

This game you introduced—are you preparing our people for battle?

Baasalt gave the mental equivalent of a chuckle. *Very good. Yes, I am. Once our people have become accustomed to thinking in terms of the possibilities of open space—instead of merely recoiling in horror at the mention of the Void—they will be ready for the next step.*

And what will that be?

Seeing the Skin-Dwellers as a resource we are not

fully using. Seeing the Skin of the World as a place that rightfully should be ours. Seeing that conquering the Void itself is not only possible . . . it is our destiny.

Feldspaar could feel the rightness of Baasalt's words.

I will follow you, he thought.

So will the rest . . .

"Doyle? Did you hear that?" Cordelia said.

"What? I didn't hear anythin'."

"Are you sure? I thought I heard a noise."

"That's generally what people do with noises."

Cordelia glared at him. "Leave the sarcasm to the experts, Doyle. I'm assuming you at least *understand* the word expert?"

"That would be a fine example right there, I'm thinkin'—"

Crash!

"That, I heard," Doyle said, jumping to his feet.

"Sounded like it came from Angel's place," Cordelia said. She glanced nervously toward the elevator Angel used to get from his living quarters to his office. "What should we do?"

"Go see what it is?" Doyle suggested.

THUMP!

"Are you *crazy?* It could be some horrible demon-monster-thingy! If it's crashing around in

Angel's place, it *has* to be some horrible demon-monster-thingy! And fending off HDMTs in the middle of the night is *not* in my job description!"

"You know, for someone halfway through a freak-out, you're pretty handy with the acronyms."

She punched him on the shoulder. "It's a gift. Now go see what it is."

"Me? I thought you just said—"

"I said it wasn't in *my* job description. Since you're the guy that gets visions, obtaining information definitely falls into *your* area. Come see me if you want paperwork filed or coffee made."

"Well, all right—" Doyle grabbed the sword Angel had been practicing with earlier off the wall and hefted it in both hands. He slid open the folding metal cage that formed the elevator door, then turned around. "But I want a fresh-brewed cup of coffee ready when I get back. Or possibly medical aid."

"I'll try to get Angel on his cell. And Doyle—be careful."

Doyle closed the cage door and hit the down button. *No problem. Just a cat or something. I can look like a hero to Cordy, and I can probably do it without making an ass of myself.*

Probably.

The lights were out, of course. He slid the cage door open and fumbled for the light switch. Nothing happened when he clicked it on.

Just a burnt-out bulb. Not a deliberately smashed light designed to set me up for the fatal heart attack I'm going to have when something reaches out of the darkness and wraps around my throat. Nope.

"Hello? Look, if you're a burglar, there's nothin' down here worth stealin'. The man doesn't even own a TV."

He took a cautious step forward into the dark, holding the sword over his head and gripping the handle tightly with both hands.

"And if you're a—horrible monster-demon-thingy, you should know I'm holdin' a piece of steel specially designed t'lop the heads off unholy creatures o' the night. Swear to God."

The voice that spoke to him wasn't audible to the ear; it echoed inside his brain, instead.

It is foolish to lie to a telepath. We are here for our brother.

"Uh-oh . . ." Doyle whispered.

Angel's cell phone rang just as Kate was finishing dessert.

"Hello?"

"Angel? Listen, you've got to get back to the office. There's something in your apartment and I don't think it's friendly."

"Where's Doyle?"

"He went down to check it out. He's—"

Angel could hear distant crashing sounds. "—*definitely* not friendly," Cordelia said.

"On my way." He hung up and swapped his phone for his wallet. "Sorry, gotta go," he told Kate. "Emergency." He tossed a few bills on the table. "Had a great time. Thanks." He turned around and bolted for the door.

Thank God, he thought.

He phoned Cordelia back as he got into the car and roared away. "I'm headed your way. Give me an update."

"Okay, well, there was a lot of crashing and banging. Oh, there's some more." Angel could hear it in the background. "Pretty sure that yelp was Doyle . . . that sounds like furniture breaking. Don't know what that muffled thump was . . . that yell was *definitely* Doyle . . . okay, I think that was your china cabinet. Wait, you don't have a china cabinet. Another, louder thump—that's weird. It almost sounded like it came from above me—

Whump!

"That one *definitely* came from overhead—"

"Cordelia, get out of the office! Now!"

There was a loud *WHUMP!* even Angel could hear . . . then nothing.

"Cordelia? Cordelia!"

Cordelia peeked up over the edge of her desk. The outer office was filled with a cloud of plaster dust from the large hole in the ceiling.

A figure stirred, then rose from the floor. The figure of a Tremblor.

"I *knew* keeping him in a cardboard box was a stupid idea!" Cordelia whispered into the phone. "He just Bugs-Bunnied his way into the office!"

"Excuse me?"

"He used his—his magic shoveling powers to rip his way through every floor between the roof and the office. Don't they have *stairs* in the middle of the Earth? He almost fell on me!"

"Cordelia, calm down. I'll be there soon. In the meantime, if you can make it outside you'll be safe."

"I don't think that's going to work, Angel. He's between me and the door—and he's just noticed me."

"Stay out of his way. He may simply want to escape."

"You're kidding, right? Well, there goes my plan to Xena his rocky butt."

You. The touch of another mind to her own.

Ohmygodlookpleasedon'thurtmeIcouldn'tpossibly beanytroubletoyouthoughyoucertainlyaremessingup MYeveningI'msorrysoanywaywecanbefriendsright???

The mental touch abruptly withdrew. Cordelia caught the faint impression that the Tremblor was . . . overwhelmed?

Doyle had always hated dodgeball.

In junior high, he'd decided that Hell consisted of an eternal game of dodgeball—except instead of sadistic jocks pelting you with large rubber balls, sadistic demons would do the same with red-hot boulders. It would go on and on, the demons making humiliating comments about how you ran like a girl, and every time you got beaned you would have to start all over again.

The one time in my life I get something absolutely dead right, he thought, *and I don't have any money on it. Figures.*

He was crouched behind Angel's overturned kitchen table, or at least what was left of it. The sword was lying on the floor beside him; at the moment it was about as useful as a flyswatter.

KRAACK!

A large hole appeared a few inches to the right of his head. The football-sized rock that had made it punched through one of Angel's kitchen cabinets as well, and probably deep into the wall after that.

How was that?

Better. You are still overcompensating for the pull of gravity. Watch this.

Doyle flattened himself just in time. The last of the table smashed apart as the next rock hit, sailing by only inches above his head. He darted to the next piece of cover, an overturned bookshelf.

Despite the fact that overhearing their conversation had probably just saved his life, Doyle really wished they'd shut up.

See? That was called a "fastball." Apparently the proper positioning of your digits can even cause the projectile to curve in midflight.

Amazing. And you learned all this from the Skin-Dweller's mind? I had no idea they knew so much.

Oh, yes. The movement of spheres through the Void occupies a great deal of their thought processes. Here's a variation they call "bowling."

Doyle groaned, but scooted to the side. A second later, a rock smashed through the middle of the bookcase at floor level.

Cordelia waited for the Tremblor to attack or run away, but it did neither. It just stood there, its shovel-shaped tail swaying back and forth slowly behind its head.

"Mr.—um—Mr. Marlboro? You can go now," Cordelia called out. "We're dropping all charges. You made parole. You get out of jail, free."

"Cordelia!" Angel said over the phone. "Don't attract his attention!"

The Tremblor quivered, then shook himself. A low rumble filled the air.

"Oops . . ." Cordelia breathed.

The rumble increased. Books fell off shelves. The desk began to jitter on the shuddering floor.

The glass partitions separating the offices shattered, as well as the windows in the outer office.

Cordelia screamed and covered her head as shards flew through the air.

And just as suddenly as it had begun, the shaking stopped.

You have destroyed me.

The Tremblor stalked forward. It stopped before Cordelia's desk. *I have looked into the Void, and the Void has looked into me. I cannot get away from it now. It is there every time I close my eyes.*

It raised both its massive, rocky fists.

And you will pay!

Its fists hammered down, smashing the desk into splinters. Cordelia scrambled as far away from it as she could, into a corner. She cut herself on broken glass and hardly noticed. She had to get away, to get outside—

She was right next to the broken window.

Without thinking, she straddled the window sill, found the thin ledge with her foot, then climbed out. She inched her way down the ledge, praying that the Tremblor would forget about her once she was gone.

The bricks beside the window exploded outward. Cordelia screamed and nearly lost her balance. The Tremblor's spade-shaped tail jutted out from the wall it had just rammed its way through.

It withdrew—and a moment later, it slammed through the wall at another spot.

This time it was a lot closer to Cordelia.

◦   ◦   ◦

Look, guys, Doyle thought as loud as he could. *There's no reason t'use me for target practice. If you want your pal, go ahead. We were gonna let him go anyway.*

There was a pause in the bombardment.

Feldspaar. Stay here with the Skin-Dweller. I will fetch Maarl.

A hulking form stomped out of the darkness, silhouetted by the light filtering through the cage of the elevator. It trudged its way over to the concrete stairs, then up them. For some reason, it came as no surprise to Doyle that the demon had a pickax sticking out of the back of its head.

"So—you're just gonna wait 'til your buddy comes back and then you'll leave, right?" Doyle called out hopefully.

Not until I try a few things. Baasalt said this was called a "knuckleball" . . .

Another rocky missile smashed into the wall.

"Wait!" Doyle yelled. "Hey, have you ever heard of something called—uh . . ." He thought desperately. *Basketball? No. Football? Worse. Golf? Introducing clubs—not a good idea. Same with tennis, badminton, cricket, polo . . .*

"—bobsledding?" Doyle asked.

Baasalt could feel the confusion and rage in Maarl's thoughts. It increased as he drew closer.

Maarl, he thought. *Maarl, it is I. Baasalt, First Warrior-Priest. Calm yourself—you are safe.*

No! I will not be calm, not ever again! All peace has been taken from me—where once was serenity and stability, all is empty chaos!

Baasalt entered the room where Maarl's thoughts emanated from. The Tremblor was punching his tail through a wall, having already made several large holes. He did not seem to care that he was gradually exposing himself to more and more of the Void.

Maarl. STOP. He broadcast as forcefully as he could.

Maarl paused. His whole body still vibrated with anger.

You have looked into the Void, Baasalt thought. *I can see it plainly.*

It has tainted me! Corrupted me!

No. It has made you stronger.

How can you think such a thing?

Because I, too, have looked into the Void.

What? No, it cannot be—you are First Warrior-Priest!

Touch my memories. See for yourself.

Maarl did so.

His body stiffened in shock as he relived Baasalt's experience—not just the memory of looking into the Void, but the memory of Baasalt's reaction to it. His initial fear had been swept away by an immense feeling of potential, of endless possibilities. It had thrilled him to the very core of his being, had given him the feeling he could do anything. The Void was still dangerous, still powerful—but it could be controlled. It could be *beaten*.

Do you see? Baasalt thought. *Do you understand?*

Maarl met his leader's eyes. *Yes,* he thought numbly. *Great Heart of the World, yes. Forgive my weakness, Baasalt. I did not have the courage to see as you did.*

You are not weak. You are strong. Can you not feel it, deep within you now? I can. You and I have faced the Void, and we are still here. We can show others our vision. We can lead them into a new era, where the Void fears us.

Baasalt held out one rocky claw. *Will you join me? Will you stand beside me in this great adventure?*

Maarl did not hesitate. He reached out and grasped Baasalt's claw with his own. *I would be honored, First Warrior-Priest.*

Good. Then let us quit this place.

They headed for the stairs.

What I need, Doyle thought, *is a plan. Specifically, a plan that doesn't involve me gettin' a rock put through my skull.*

He was running out of cover; there wasn't much

left of the bookshelf he was currently hiding behind. The Tremblor, though, seemed to have no shortage of rocks.

If I could just get t'the stairs, I could get outta here. But there's no way Roger Clemens here is gonna let me do that. Doyle's eyes had adjusted to the darkness; the light coming from the elevator cage was enough to let him make out a few details. The Tremblors had come in through the tunnels Angel normally used, and they'd brought a pile of rocks with them.

Doyle's eyes flickered over the wreckage of the apartment. He'd just had an idea—now, if only what he was looking for hadn't been smashed into bits . . .

There. Of course, it had to be lying between him and the Quake demon—and he had no idea if it had been broken.

Ah, well. Never said no to a gamble before.

Doyle dived out from behind the bookshelf, grabbed the camera and held it up. He fumbled for the button while the Tremblor cocked one massive arm behind its head.

The flash went off. The blinded Tremblor bellowed, let fly and missed Doyle by six inches.

Doyle sprinted for the stairs.

They met at around the halfway point.

One moment Doyle was barreling up the stairs at

full speed; the next he was lying flat on his back, on a landing between floors. After a few groggy seconds, he realized he'd run into something at full tilt and rebounded.

He looked up into the face of a Tremblor.

"Uh," Doyle said.

"Doyle! *Get out of the way!*"

Angel's voice.

Doyle threw himself, headfirst, back down the stairs.

Angel launched himself at the Tremblor, delivering a flying kick to the demon's chest. Off-balance on the steps, it tumbled forward and crashed into the other one. They both bounced off the wall and continued downward.

Falling down a flight of concrete steps was not the most pleasant experience Doyle had ever gone through, but he didn't have time to complain. He had other things to worry about, like half a ton of living rock tumbling toward him like an angry avalanche.

He hit the bottom and rolled clear. An instant later, two Tremblors smashed into the spot he'd just vacated.

Doyle got to his feet, trying to ignore the pain of his bruised body. As long as Angel was here, they had a chance.

The Tremblors disentangled themselves and got to their feet as well.

"Angel?" Doyle said hopefully.

No response.

"Angel!" The cry came from above.

"Cordelia," Angel said. He turned and sprinted up the steps.

He ran into the office and stopped. There was a huge hole in the ceiling, all the glass was smashed and Cordelia's desk was a pile of kindling. There were also a half-dozen large holes punched in one wall—and no sign of Cordelia.

"Angel!" The voice seemed to be coming from outside. "Get me down from here!"

Angel stuck his head out the window. Cordelia was about fifteen feet away, standing on a narrow ledge with her arms flat against the wall. She looked terrified.

"Cordelia, I'm here—are you all right?"

"Am I all right? What does it look like? Get me down!"

"Can you hang on just a moment?"

"What? No! Where are you going? *Angel!*"

"They're gone," Doyle said. "Didn't seem too interested in me once they had their buddy. Can't say I'm disappointed."

Angel looked around the remains of his apartment. "Now I know how the Serpentene feel," he said.

"Except your pockets are not quite as deep."

"I'll worry about that later. Right now, we have an assistant to rescue."

"Just don't look down," Doyle said.

"Why does everyone always say that when someone is stuck someplace high? Do you think I'm *stupid*? Of course I'm not going to—" She looked down. *"EEEEEEE!"*

"Cordelia!" Angel snapped. "Look at me. That's right. Now move toward me, slowly."

"What do you mean, move toward you? What are you waiting for? *You* move toward *me!*"

"All right . . ." Angel took the rope Doyle handed him and climbed out on the ledge. He started inching closer to Cordelia.

"What are you *doing?*" Cordelia demanded.

"I'm—saving you?"

"Right! So make with the wings already!"

"Wings?"

"Okay, maybe you don't have wings, but do whatever you do—flap your trenchcoat or something!"

"Cordelia, I can't fly."

"What? What do you mean, you can't fly? You're a vampire! Vampires can always fly!"

"That's a common misconception. We don't turn into bats, either."

"I am *never* going to get all these rules straight . . ."

Angel stretched out his arm. Cordelia edged toward it—and stepped on a loose bit of rubble. It shifted just enough to make her lose her balance.

She fell.

CHAPTER NINE

"You're stronger than you look," Cordelia told Doyle. "I'm surprised you could haul both of us up."

"I'm just glad Angel managed to snag you before you hit the ground," Doyle said. "Though it's really Angel's fashion sense we have to thank for the happy endin'."

Angel was examining the armpit of his coat critically. "I think you popped a seam," he muttered.

"Well, I had t'grab somethin'. A handful of trenchcoat was the best I could do. Anyway, if anybody should be complainin', it's me," Doyle said. "You nearly Wiley Coyote'ed me with that stunt with the Boulder Brothers." He dumped the broken glass off a chair and sat down. "And then there's the one the Tremblors pulled on me. Seems they have a trick that none of your books mentioned, probably because they were all written before Abner Doubleday was born."

"Who's Abner Doubleday?" Cordelia said. She opened the first-aid kit and took out some peroxide. She started dabbing it on a cut on Doyle's forehead.

"The guy who invented baseball," Doyle said. "Seems the Tremblors are big fans, except they prefer t'use stones the size of cannonballs instead of the ol' horsehide. That, and they seem t'be a little unclear on the difference between 'pitching' and 'mass destruction.'"

"They threw rocks at you?" Angel asked.

"Okay—when *you* say it, it sounds stupid. When you're on the other end of a bowling ball from Hell, the situation looks a little grimmer . . ."

"The question now is, will the Tremblors change their plans?" Angel said. "The one they freed will warn them we know where they'll strike next."

"If they're gonna go through with this Crushing of Souls ritual, they may not have a choice," Doyle said. "Ow!"

"Don't be such a wimp," Cordelia said. "Peroxide can't cause blindness, can it?"

"They may move their agenda up," Angel said. "We should stake out the graveyard tonight."

"I hate to be a naysayer," Doyle said, "but so far, we haven't exactly been doin' great against these guys. Now that they know we're comin', we don't even have the advantage of surprise. We need an edge."

"We might have one," Angel said. "We'll make a stop on the way. The equipment I ordered is ready."

"One thing I don't understand," Doyle said as they pulled up to the curb and parked. "Who exactly are we protectin' in a graveyard?"

"Good question," Angel said as he got out. "Unless the Tremblors are planning on raising the dead, I'd guess it was someone who works here. Probably the caretaker."

There was a big iron gate at the entrance, sealed with a chain and padlock. "Doyle?" Angel said.

Doyle went to work, and a few moments later the lock was open. They went in.

As they walked up the path, Doyle said, "Okay, so far we've got an airline hostess, a firefighter and a lifeguard. Like you said, they all put their lives at risk from the element they're close to. A caretaker doesn't really seem t'be in the same ballpark."

"Depends on how you look at it," Angel said. "Earth is the most important element in the ritual; it's the one that the new Tremblors' bodies are made out of. The caretaker of a graveyard is responsible for the bodies of thousands of people, interned within the Earth itself. Symbolically, that makes him or her the maternal figure, the one that protects the unborn."

"Still, not exactly a dangerous job," Doyle pointed out.

"You wouldn't think so, would you?" a strong voice said behind them. "No sudden moves, please."

Angel and Doyle stopped and turned around slowly.

A black man in his sixties stood there. He had silver hair and wore a faded plaid shirt, brown pants and a baggy brown sweater. He had a shotgun cradled in one arm.

"You don't look like vandals," the man said. "So I'm guessing graverobbers. Well, I am sick and tired of bodies disappearing. You can just get the hell out of my graveyard—or I'll use you to fill a few recent vacancies."

"Uh, you've got it all wrong," Angel said. "We're not graverobbers or vandals."

"And why should I believe you?" the man demanded.

"We're not carrying shovels or spray paint, are we?" Angel pointed out. "And we don't have a wheelbarrow. Don't graverobbers usually have a wheelbarrow?"

"Besides," added Doyle, "look at how we're dressed. Okay, well, how *he's* dressed. Not exactly clothes for diggin' in the dirt."

The man eyed them suspiciously. "All right then, what *are* you doing here?"

"I'm a security consultant," Angel said. Moving slowly, he took a business card out of his pocket and handed it over. "I was—hired by the city to look into the recent rash of disappearances."

The man took the card and glanced at it. He frowned, but lowered the shotgun. "Why didn't they tell me you were coming?"

"I can't say for sure," Angel answered. "Maybe they figured a surprise inspection might produce the best results."

The man snorted. "It's like that, is it? Well, I don't have anything to hide. You want to look around or ask me some questions, go ahead."

"How about a proper introduction, first. I'm Angel. This is my associate, Doyle." Angel held out his hand.

After a moment's hesitation, the man shook it. "I'm Harold Worthington. Call me Harry."

"Okay, Harry," Angel said. "We don't want to get in your way. Is it all right if we just—follow you around for a while?"

"I suppose. I can show you the most recently disturbed sites, but then I have some work to do. Can't spend the whole night playing tour guide."

"We'd appreciate that."

Harry led them between rows of tombstones. "It's

about time the city decided to send someone to check things out. I've been telling them for years about the strange goings-on out here, and nobody ever took me seriously. Thought I was crazy."

"What kinds of things?" Doyle asked nervously.

"Fresh graves being disturbed, tombstones knocked over, trails of slime that disappear when the sun hits them—all sorts of weirdness. Some of it's just kids fooling around, but I got my own theory about the rest."

"And what theory would that be?" Angel asked.

Harry stopped and turned around. He studied Angel, then shook his head. "Forget it. You'd just think I was crazy, too. Tell you what—you look around, you tell *me* what you think's going on."

Harry continued on his way. Angel dropped back a little and whispered to Doyle, "Guy's pretty sharp."

"Yeah, and I take back what I said about this not being a dangerous job. A graveyard in L.A.? Geez, he's probably seen everything from demons to mad scientists . . ."

Harry stopped at a grave with a new headstone. It was obviously a new grave, the flowers on it still fresh. The dirt bore the all-too-distinctive eruptive pattern that told Angel someone or something had recently clawed their way up from below.

"Get a couple of these a year," Harry said.

"Always the same. Someone young, someone murdered—though sometimes they claim it's suicide—and buried for a couple days. Within a week, the grave looks like this. Now what do you figure could be the cause?"

"Uh—moles?" Angel said.

Harry looked at Angel. "Moles. Right. The kind with big, sharp pointy teeth."

"Most people don't realize moles are actually carnivorous," Doyle said. "Sure, they usually eat bugs and such, but a big tasty corpse is hard t'resist. It's like a free underground buffet."

"But they can also be dangerous," Angel interjected. "Even attack people. You should be very careful."

"Oh, I am. That's why I carry this." Harry patted the barrel of his shotgun.

"That—won't neccesarily work," Angel said carefully. "Against . . . certain breeds of mole."

"Angel," Doyle warned. "Come on. I'm sure the man knows all about moles."

"And what would you suggest?" Harry asked. "For these certain breeds of mole?"

"It depends. Some varieties have an aversion to silver. With others, it's wood. Sometimes, something as simple as specially-treated water can do the trick."

Harry studied Angel for a moment. A smile rose

slowly on his wrinkled face. "Silver's expensive. Wood's only useful in certain cases. And I'm too old to lug gallons of water around." He dug in the pocket of his sweater and pulled out a shotgun shell. "Make these myself. Finely ground communion wafer mixed in with the buckshot. Works against damn near anything."

"That's very . . . creative," Angel said with a tentative smile. "I guess you can take care of yourself."

"Been doing it for sixty-odd years," Harry said. "I guess I can last a few more."

He suddenly slapped a hand to the back of his neck. "Mosquito season's here," Harry grumbled. "Damn bloodsuckers . . ."

After that, Harry warmed up a little. He showed them a few more disturbed graves, including one covered with gang graffiti, then invited them back to his cottage for a hot drink. "Take the chill off your bones," he said. "Mine, too."

The caretaker's cottage was in the middle of the graveyard, a small Spanish-style bungalow with red clay tiles on the roof. Inside it was neat and clean, with a small living room adjoined by a kitchenette and a single bedroom. Old movie posters covered the walls, all from westerns: *Stagecoach, High Noon, Shane.*

Angel and Doyle sat side-by-side on the couch,

while Harry busied himself making hot chocolate. "That's a nasty bruise you've got on your forehead," he commented to Doyle.

"Baseball injury," Doyle said. "Got hit by a foul ball. *Extremely* foul."

"One in three hundred thousand," Harry said.

"Pardon me?" Angel said.

"That's the chance of getting hit by a baseball—at a major league game, anyway," Harry said. "Statistics are a hobby of mine. Started out just being curious about how folks passed on, and it kind of grew from there."

"Really?" Doyle said, brightening. "Odds-makin' happens to be a bit of a pastime with myself. For instance: winnin' a lottery in California—fourteen million to one."

"Chance of being hit by lightning in any given week," Harry said. "Two hundred and fifty million to one."

"Chances of making twenty-eight straight passes at a crap table," Doyle countered. "Forty million to one. Actually happened at the Desert Inn in Vegas in 1950; the guy throwin' the dice obviously didn't trust his own luck, because he bet conservatively. Only walked away with seven hundred and fifty bucks—though one of the Marx Brothers was tableside and pulled in twenty-eight grand."

"Groucho?" asked Angel.

"Nah, Zeppo. That guy got more luck than he deserved."

Harry stirred the pot of hot chocolate slowly, and added a little milk. "Chance of the Earth being wiped out by a meteorite in the next fifty years—one million, two hundred thousand to one."

"Gettin' dealt a Royal Flush on the openin' hand—six hundred forty-nine thousand, seven hundred and thirty-nine to one."

Harry set out mugs on the counter. He carefully poured the hot chocolate into them from the pot. "Odds of being murdered while living in the good old U.S. of A., in any given year: one in twelve thousand. Odds of being murdered here over the course of a lifetime—one in ninety-nine."

"I see why you carry the shotgun," Angel said.

Harry chuckled as he put the mugs on a tray. "Yeah, at my age I'm just about due. Of course, statistically speaking, what I do isn't considered high-risk; cabbies and convenience-store clerks stand the biggest chance of being murdered on the job, followed by truckers and gas station attendants. Now, what does that say about our society—when doing something as simple as driving someone from one place to another or selling them junk food can get you killed?"

"Especially between midnight and four A.M.," Angel said. "Graveyard shift—so to speak."

Harry nodded thoughtfully, then brought the mugs over on a tray and handed one to Angel and one to Doyle. He took the last one himself before sinking down into an easy chair. "Well, at least the economy's doing okay. Chance of getting shot always goes up when the dollar dives. Jumps from about fifty-eight percent of murder victims to sixty-five."

"That really cheers *me* up," Angel said.

"Thing is, you can use statistics to prove just about anything," Harry said. "Can't live your life by them, though. Life has a way of doing the unexpected—sometimes even the impossible." He fixed a steady gaze at Angel. "But then, I think you already know that."

"I've . . . had my share of unusual experiences," Angel admitted.

"Uh-huh. Something tells me that's an understatement."

"Look, Harry, I'm going to level with you as best I can. I think you may be in danger."

"From what? The things that creep around out there?" Harry snorted. "They don't bother me—and for the most part, I don't bother them. The city pays me to dig graves and maintain the grounds, not play monster-hunter."

"It's a little more complicated than that," Doyle said. "See, the people we think might threaten you are sort of—"

"—a cult," Angel interjected. "And you know people like that aren't exactly rational. They've been kidnapping people connected to the four elements; so far they've got an airline hostess, a firefighter and a lifeguard. As near as we can tell—you're next."

"Something tells me you boys don't work for the city." Harry took a sip of his hot chocolate.

"Not exactly," Angel said. "But we are trying to stop this cult. I'm hoping you'll let us keep an eye on you for the next twenty-four hours. Our information indicates that's when they'll strike."

"What did you have in mind?"

"Doyle can stay in here with you. I'll patrol outside. We'll stay in touch via cell phone."

Harry put down his mug and leaned back. He folded his hands in front of him and glanced over at Doyle. "I know I'm going to regret this, but I have one question I need to ask. I'm pretty sure what the answer will be, so don't even think about lying to me."

"Yeah?" Doyle said.

"Do you play gin?"

Angel prowled through the graveyard, alone. He'd left Harry and Doyle playing cards for a nickel a point.

He'd spent a lot of time in graveyards, once. Hiding out in them, bringing his kills to them. Not because he had to—he slept in a bed, not a coffin—but because it was part of the game, because it terrified his victims even more. Ever since he'd regained his soul, he'd avoided them. Too many bad memories.

And then came Buffy.

The Slayer. He'd been sent to help her, to watch her back. He'd wound up in graveyards more than once while doing that—and had become more than her ally. Now, walking between the tombstones held a bittersweet quality, reminding him of both better and worse times.

The problem was, there were so many more bad memories than good.

He read the markers to pass the time. *Beloved Son. A Good Father. Gone Before Her Time. We Will Meet Again In Heaven.* Angel wondered if that would be true for him and Buffy—would they eventually be together in the afterlife? Or was his soul beyond redemption?

Maybe I just won't die, he thought to himself. *If I eat right, exercise regularly, stay away from the sun, I'm probably good for . . . well, ever.* Somehow, that didn't cheer him up.

He kept walking and reading. *Rest In Peace. Died Too Young. God Called Her Home.*

Peace. Young. Her home. The words seemed to mock him.

Cordelia was right. I just can't seem to pass on the angst . . . And what do we have here—the graves of small children? Boy, this is better than Christmas . . .

He continued his patrol. If he was *really* lucky, he'd be attacked by some undead creature of the night.

Unfortunately, most unholy terrors seemed to have taken the evening off. Over the next few hours, Angel spotted nothing but a few coyotes outside the fence, who looked at him with knowing yellow eyes and then disappeared into the night.

His cell phone rang. "Doyle?"

"Yeah. Harry just went to bed."

"Pretty quiet out here."

"Well, it's not exactly Mardi Gras in here, either. Although it's turnin' out to be just as expensive."

Angel smiled. "Harry taught you a few things about gin, did he?"

"It was more in the nature of a refresher course, but the fees were definitely pro level. I convinced him t'take an IOU, which I'm hopin' he'll forget about once we save his life. We *are* gonna save his life, right?"

"I guarantee it," Angel said grimly.

"Say, there's somethin' I don't quite get," Doyle said. "I can understand you keepin' the whole I'm-a-vampire-*and*-a-good-guy thing quiet; I can even understand why you might want to warn him about vamps without soundin' like a lunatic. But once it seemed obvious he knew what was goin' on, you didn't give him the straight goods on the Tremblors. Why not?"

"Doyle, you and I live in a certain kind of world. We deal with vampires, with demons, with poltergeists and witchcraft. Buffy even got attacked by a killer robot, once. But just because we take those things for granted doesn't mean other people do—even people who've been exposed to them."

He leaned against the wall of a mausoleum. "Most people think vampires are a myth. Once they find out they're not, they have to adjust their worldview. That's a big thing; it shakes up their whole belief system. Some people can't handle it, while others adapt. Harry's obviously adapted.

"But as you and I know, there's more than vampires out there. Making the leap from vampires to werewolves isn't that hard; most people kind of lump them together anyway. But it still has an impact—an aftershock, if you like.

"Now add the existence of a race of demons. Another aftershock. Add a whole slew of demon races. Each one has a cumulative effect."

"I see what you're gettin' at. Sooner or later, somebody's whole view of reality collapses."

"Exactly. Now, I don't know how many shocks

Harry's had, or what kind of philosophy he's structured to justify the existence of vampires—he might not even see them as supernatural beings. But I didn't know how far I could push it. If we deliver one shock too many, his belief structure might fall apart—and the most common way of dealing with that is denial. If that happened, he'd probably refuse to talk to us. I couldn't take the chance."

"So you fed him something semi-plausible, and let his own beliefs fill in the details. And here I thought you were just bein' your usual mysterious self."

"Me? Mysterious? Never."

"Hey, I just thought of somethin'. If bein' exposed to all this world-shakin' information destroys your sense of what's what, then how come you and I aren't locked up in a rubber room somewhere?"

"You know, I ask myself that very question every day. . . ."

Emilio Maldonado used to have questions. He would ask them of God, the same ones every day, and God never answered. God, it seemed, did not wish to talk to him.

But that no longer mattered, because he had found someone who would.

Emilio Maldonado was a geologist, and he was

good at his job. At least he had been, until The Event. That was how he thought of it now: The Event. Like a seismic event, but in capital letters. The disaster that had torn apart his life like a cheap jigsaw puzzle and scattered the pieces far and wide.

He could still see the pieces, but they no longer fit together. And for the longest time, the most important piece of all had been missing.

But no more.

The small apartment he lived in was on the second floor of an old motel in the Plaza district. He was close to Olvera Street, and sometimes he walked there to buy a fresh *churro* dusted with sugar or listen to the mariachis play for the tourists; Hector had always loved both.

Most nights though, he stayed in.

Headlights shone through the window and winked off the hundreds of tequila bottles stacked against one wall. They were balanced one on top of another, from floor to ceiling, fixed in place with glue. All of them were empty, except for a shriveled, dead worm in the bottom. Emilio had emptied them all himself.

Other than the bottles, the room was small and undistinguished. There was little in it other than the faded couch Emilio sat on and a television he no longer bothered to watch. He had better things to do with his time. Indeed, he had much time to make up for. That was why he kept the tequila bottles, though he no longer drank; as a reminder of how much time he had wasted.

The wall of bottles had originally been intended for a different purpose. He had finished the first bottle the night of The Event, drank it himself, and when he had got to the bottom the sight of the small, dead worm seemed the cruelest joke in the world. He couldn't bear to eat it, nor could he throw it away. He had placed the empty bottle on a shelf where he could see it every night, and every night he added another. Over time, it developed from an uncontrollable habit to a morbid fascination: how many bottles of tequila would it take to completely destroy a man? It was a question he became determined to answer.

He had lived in a much bigger house then, a much nicer house. Now that house was just another puzzle piece, no longer connected to the others: his wife, his possessions, his old job. All scattered. When he lost his house, the bottles were the only thing he took with him.

It didn't matter. The one piece of the puzzle that he cared about, the one he'd lost first, had come back to him. Now the bottles symbolized not destruction, but triumph; he had beaten them. He had beaten Death itself.

He cradled Hector's picture in both hands.

Hector had died from a gunshot wound, an innocent bystander caught in a drive-by shooting. He had been ten years old.

The picture was an eight-by-ten in a cheap gilt frame. Hector posed in his soccer uniform, one foot on a ball, a park in the background. He was at least fourteen.

"Hector," Emilio whispered. He rubbed the frame and concentrated.

The photo came to life, as if it were a TV screen and not glossy paper. Hector smiled at him. "Hello, Poppy," he said. "Good to see you."

"It's good to see you, too, son," Emilio said. "Tell me about your day. . . ."

"Morning," Harry said.

Doyle sat bolt upright on the couch. "I wasn't sleepin', swear t'God . . . oh, it's you, Harry. Sorry." Doyle yawned and stretched. "What time is it?"

"About a half-hour before dawn. I like to get an early start on the day." Harry began to make coffee. "Your partner still outside?"

"Yeah, he prefers to go it alone. I should check in with him, though." Doyle picked up his cell phone and punched in Angel's number.

"Doyle? Everything all right?"

"Peachy. Harry's up and rarin' t'go. Looks like our friends are a no-show."

"Nothing to report out here, either. I'm coming in."

"Gotcha." Doyle disconnected.

Harry offered them breakfast, which Angel turned down and Doyle accepted.

"I notice you keep looking at your watch," Harry observed as he poured Angel a cup of coffee. "Got an early appointment?"

"Yes," Angel said. "An extremely important one." He glared at Doyle, who was finishing his third slice of toast.

"What? I don't remember—oh, right. That *sunrise* appointment." He gobbled the last piece and got up. "I guess we better be hittin' the road."

"Actually, *I'll* be going," Angel said. "Doyle will stay with you, if that's all right."

"If he doesn't mind following an old man around all day."

"Are you sure?" Doyle said. "I don't mind—but so far, these cultists have only attacked at night."

Angel took a sip of his coffee. "I don't want to take any chances."

Doyle shrugged. "Fine by me, I guess."

"I checked the grounds out pretty thoroughly last night. I don't have to be at my appointment for another—" Angel checked his watch. "—twenty-two minutes, so I'll give you a quick rundown on possible problem areas."

"Sure thing." Doyle glanced over at Harry, who was just heading into the bathroom. When the door closed, Doyle leaned over and said to Angel, "Problem areas? I thought everything underneath our feet was a problem area when it comes to these guys."

"Just trying to be thorough," Angel said. "If the Tremblors are going to attack during the day, they'll probably pick a covered area to surface in, like a mausoleum. I just want you to be aware of which ones are most likely."

Harry came out of the bathroom. "Okay, I've got some graves to dig; hope you don't mind loud machinery."

"Lead the way," Doyle said.

The backhoe was stored in a shed behind the bungalow. Harry unlocked the door, but Angel stuck his head and looked around before letting him enter. Landscaping and gardening tools hung along the wall, while a riding mower and a beat-up orange backhoe took up most of the floor space. The floor itself was concrete, and seemed undisturbed; Angel even checked under the vehicles to make sure they weren't concealing tunnel entrances.

"All clear," Angel said.

Harry climbed onto the backhoe and started it up with a roar. He backed out of the shed, turned the machine around, then began trundling down the road at a sedate pace. Angel and Doyle followed him on foot, Angel pointing out various crypts to Doyle that he thought the Tremblors might use.

Harry turned the backhoe onto the grounds. He stopped in front of a rectangular plot outlined in white plastic tape stretched between four sticks.

He geared down, then motioned Doyle over. "You mind getting rid of those markers for me?"

"Sure."

Once the markers were gone Harry got right to work, biting into the ground with the bucket and depositing scoops of earth beside the hole. Within minutes he had a trench dug six feet deep.

"—And watch the bushes beside the north wall," Angel said.

Doyle sighed. "Yeah, yeah, I got it. Don't you think you should be toddlin' off? You're about thirty seconds away from being a crispy critter."

Angel glanced at his watch. "I've still got a minute or two. As long as I can make it to the car I'll be okay."

Chunk!

The backhoe whined and sputtered. "Hell!" Harry said. He put the motor in idle, then climbed down from the seat. "Damn thing's caught on something."

Before Doyle or Angel could stop him, he'd scrambled down into the hole itself.

"No!" Angel shouted, and jumped in after him.

"What do you think you're doing, boy?" Harry asked. He was crouched beside the bucket, which was jammed into the wall of the pit. Dirt crumbled around the edges of the massive boulder it had failed to dislodge.

"Uh—" Angel said. "I was just making sure you . . . didn't hurt yourself."

"I told you before, I can take care of myself."

Behind Harry, two rocky claws reached out from the dirt wall.

Angel had no time to think. He grabbed Harry under each arm and tossed him skyward as hard as he could, out of the grave and into the first rays of the rising sun. From the cursing Angel heard, Harry landed on Doyle.

The Tremblor emerged fully from the wall of dirt, revealing the tunnel behind it. It was the one Angel had pickaxed in the head—either that, or he'd started a trend.

"Doesn't that *hurt*?" Angel asked.

Not as much as this will.

Two more rocky claws shot up from beneath Angel, and four more from behind him. They grabbed him by the ankles, the shoulders and the arms.

When Harry came flying out of the pit, Doyle didn't have time to get out of the way. He tried to make the gravedigger's landing as soft as possible, but both of them went down in a heap with the breath knocked out of them.

Doyle didn't waste time trying to get untangled. He got an arm free, fished in the pocket of his coat and pulled out one of the items he and Angel had picked up on the way over. Then, of course, he had to get the damn thing lit.

"Angel!" he called out. *"Incoming!"*

When the magnesium flare dropped into the hole, Angel knew he had a chance.

All three Tremblors immediately released their grip, instinctively covering their eyes and filling Angel's mind with a soundless shout of pain. Angel knew bright light couldn't actually damage them, but it could give him the opportunity to fight back.

The spikes that snapped out of his wrist gauntlets and into his hands weren't the usual wooden stakes. They were specialized pieces of mountaineering equipment, diamond-tipped pitons with recoilless explosive charges to drive them into even the hardest rock. Angel had ordered them from a shop that specialized in extreme sports, and he'd had them customized even further.

He whirled and struck, slamming the pitons into the chests of the nearest two Quake demons and activating the charges. Both spikes penetrated deeply with a loud *Whump!*

Angel threw himself into a corner of the pit and covered his head. An instant later the larger, secondary charges went off.

Chunks of rock flew. Gravel and dirt showered down. The air was filled with dust and smoke.

Angel raised his head cautiously. The two Tremblors he'd land-mined were still standing, but both had large craters in their chests. Neither was moving.

"Two down," Angel muttered.

And two to go.

CHAPTER TEN

Doyle was torn. On the one hand, he knew he should get Harry as far away as possible; on the other, he didn't want to leave Angel alone fighting an unknown number of Quake demons.

"Doyle!" Angel shouted. "Get Harry out of here, *now!*"

That decided him. He pulled Harry to his feet and got him moving.

He'll be all right, Doyle thought as they ran. *Angel can take care of himself.*

Angel wasn't doing so well.

He had no room to maneuver, he was outnumbered, and he'd used up his only two weapons. With the sun risen, he couldn't even run. While the flare burned he had a slight edge, but that ended when the Tremblor that had grabbed him from below seized the flare instead and pulled it underground, extinguishing its light.

The one with the pick in its head charged him.

He evaded its first few swipes, but then the ground began to shake. Angel saw that the other one had risen from the floor of the pit and was squatting with its hands against the ground.

Now off-balance as well, the next punch caught Angel square in the face. He staggered into the arm of the backhoe. Another punch knocked him to his knees.

Suddenly, his head was clamped between two rocky claws. His vision began to shake violently . . . and then there was only blackness.

"How long are we supposed to stay up here?" Harry asked.

He and Doyle were on the bungalow's roof. It was the only place Doyle could think of to go that the Tremblors wouldn't follow.

"I don't know," Doyle said. "Somethin's wrong. Angel should of kicked their rocky tails by now. Look, you stay here; I'm gonna go check on the battlefield."

He lowered the aluminum ladder they'd hauled up after themselves and clambered down. He half-expected hands made of glossy black stone to thrust up from the ground and grab his ankles.

He jogged back to the gravesite. "Angel?" he called out.

No response. Doyle peered down into the open grave.

It was empty.

"Uh, Cordelia?" Doyle said into his cell phone. "We got a problem."

"Doyle? Do you *know* how early it is? This isn't one of those I've-been-up-all-night-drinking-and-I-love-you calls, is it?"

"What? No, of course not. It's just that, well . . ."

"Well, what?"

"I sort of . . . lost Angel."

There was a pause.

"What," Cordelia said evenly, "do you mean, you *lost* Angel?"

"In the sense of temporarily misplaced."

"Well, why are you talking to me? Go *find* him!"

"That's gonna be kinda tricky. Unless you're a lot better at shoveling than I am."

"Oh, *no*," Cordelia gasped. "The Tremblors got him?"

"Apparently. I was busy savin' victim number four, and when I got back he was gone."

"Doyle, what are we going to *do*?"

"Cordy, don't worry. I've got a plan. Look, I'm goin' back t'the office; meet me there as soon as you can." He hung up.

He wished he had the slightest idea what to do next.

Angel awoke to the sound of his heels bumping against the ground. He realized he was being dragged by the back of his collar through a tunnel in complete darkness. There was a chuffing sound coming from past his feet he couldn't quite identify; after a few moments he figured it out as being the sound of earth collapsing. The Tremblors were sealing up the tunnel behind them as they went—and he had no idea how long he'd been unconscious, or how far underground they were. For now, he was at their mercy.

I see your thoughts are active again. Good. You can walk.

The Tremblor released Angel's collar and he dropped to the ground. He got to his feet slowly. "Where are you taking me?"

To the Grounding. They will decide your fate.

"Just the people I wanted to talk to. Lead the way."

That's exactly what I intend to do.

Angel followed the sound of shuffling footsteps. Behind him, the earth continued to fall in on itself.

❖ ❖ ❖

When Cordelia got to the office, Doyle was already there. He was in Angel's office, staring at the map Angel had stuck up on the wall. There was still broken glass everywhere.

"Doyle? What are you doing?"

"Lookin' for inspiration."

Cordelia threw her bag down on Angel's desk. "I thought you said you had a plan?"

"Yeah, well, my plan was to come here, look through Angel's notes and steal *his* plan. So far, all I have is this map and a bunch of push-pins."

"You better come up with something quick. Angel's depending on us."

"I know, I know. Okay, let's pretend we're him. How would he go about rescuin' somebody from a bunch of demons?"

"First thing he'd do is find their clubhouse." Cordelia dumped some glass off a chair and sat down.

"Right, except I'm pretty sure he'd call it a lair."

"Whatever. Then he'd get something big and sharp and go hack them to bits. Simple."

Doyle rubbed his temples. "Let's back that up a step, shall we? First we gotta locate the club—the lair."

"Okay. How?"

"Well, we know it's underground. That's a start. And . . . and we know the other locations where the

Tremblors have struck." Doyle pointed to the map. "See—the push-pins."

"Great."

They both stared at the map for a moment.

"Now what?" Cordelia asked.

"Give me a second, willya?" Doyle stared hard at the map. Angel had drawn a triangle connecting three of the points: the firehouse, the lifeguard station and the flight attendant's residence. There was a fourth point now, just off to the right: the graveyard. It didn't quite match up with the others, though; if he connected all the pins, it just gave him a lopsided rectangle.

"Wait!" Cordelia said, excited. "You're not connecting them right—look!" She grabbed a pencil from Angel's desk and drew a line between two of the points, then two more angled lines branching away from the first pin. It formed a perfect arrow.

"There!" Cordelia said triumphantly. "That's where the lair is!"

"Cordy, d'you really think demons commit crimes that point out their secret headquarters? With an *arrow*?"

"It was *your* idea, Doyle."

"Yeah, but . . . I was lookin' for somethin' a little more *mystical*, y'know? Not a freeway sign . . ."

Cordelia shrugged. "Okay then—what kind of pattern do *you* see?"

"I don't." Doyle scowled. "It's that one point that's throwin' everythin' off. It's almost as if there's a point *missin'* . . ."

Doyle took a pin and added it to the left of the triangle, across from the fourth one. He looked at it for a moment, then grinned and took the pencil from Cordy.

He connected the five points in a continuous line without lifting the pencil from the map. When he was done, he'd formed a five-pointed star—a pentagram.

"Bruce Wayne, eat your heart out," he said.

Two hundred and forty sunless years had given Angel better-than-normal night vision, but he was still glad to see a faint orange glow of light ahead.

The tunnel emptied into a low-ceilinged chamber. It seemed to be constructed rather than natural; the walls were a combination of craggy rock and hard-packed earth. Oddly shaped columns of stone were spaced evenly around a low-lipped crater in the center of the room. The orange glow was coming from the crater; a pool of molten rock there threw off both light and intense heat.

Baasalt. You have returned. The voice that echoed inside Angel's head was deep and sonorous. *But this is not the Fourth sacrifice we were told of.*

"That's right," Angel said. He saw that the columns were actually Tremblors encased in stone.

He could just barely make out the shapes of their bodies and faces in the rock. "You've made a mistake. I'm not a gravedigger."

No. You are a vampire, Baasalt thought. *Is this not so?*

"Well, yes—"

You have the scent of one who spends a great deal of time below the surface.

"I use tunnels to move around during the day, but—"

You were dead and buried at some point?

"It was only three days—"

Close enough. You will suffice.

Baasalt. It was the other mind that spoke—Angel realized it had to be one of the ones embedded in the columns. *This is—unprecedented. The Fourth must balance the other three: one who braves flame, one who braves water, one who braves the Void— and one who cares for the earth. This one is a warrior, not a caregiver.*

He is a creature of the earth, Great Batholith, Baasalt countered. *That is sufficient for the ritual.*

But what sort of Tremblor will be born of four warriors?

A new kind. One that will not be content to hide inside the Body of the World and play games. One that will seek new experiences, new challenges. New territory.

There was a long silence.

"It seems," Angel said, "that there's a difference of opinion as far as my suitability goes. In a situation as critical as this one, you really should err on the side of caution. And—I'm nobody's sacrifice."

He lunged for Baasalt, and grabbed the pickax sticking out of the Tremblor's head. He yanked with all his strength and pulled it out.

(!!!!!!!!!!!!!) Baasalt's telepathic scream was like a lightning bolt through Angel's head. Stunned, he dropped the pickax and fell to his knees.

Baasalt, thought the Batholith. *Are you able to function?*

I . . . survive, came Baasalt's reply. *Though I cannot say the same about the two warrior-priests this one ended. Do not let their destruction be in vain.*

You slew two warrior-priests? Even though his brain felt numb, Angel could tell this was directed at him.

"I was protecting your so-called Fourth," Angel managed. "And I'm not going to let you murder the other three, either."

He is a protector, the Batholith mused. *Perhaps not quite a caregiver . . . but you are correct, Baasalt. He will suffice. Take him to the others.*

The First Warrior-Priest hauled Angel to his feet and took him away.

❖   ❖   ❖

"Are you sure this'll work?" Cordelia asked for the fifth time.

Doyle sighed. They were on the freeway, on their way to Appletree Estates. "For the last time, Cordy, I don't know. It makes sense, though, don't it?"

"It just seems kind of . . . goofy." Cordelia shrugged.

"Yeah, well, so does usin' somethin' you put in pasta sauce to drive away the undead, and that seems to work just fine."

"What about what Angel said? About the Serpentene not mentioning their involvement with Wolfram and Hart?"

"That bothers me, too," Doyle admitted. "But we can't pull off this plan by ourselves."

Galvin met them at the door. His eyes were heavy and his hair slightly rumpled. "I'm sorry, I'm still not quite awake," he said apologetically as he let them in. "Come on downstairs, I've got some Jamaican Blue Mountain brewing."

Once in Galvin's place, Doyle explained the situation. "I think I know how to beat these guys, but I'm gonna need your help."

"Whatever you need is yours," Galvin said.

"That's what I was hopin' you'd say. I understand you've got some studio connections . . ."

They put Angel in another cave, and sealed the entrance with a boulder. It was pitch dark.

"Are you a doctor?" said a woman's voice.

"No, but I am a friend," Angel answered.

A light flared in the darkness. It came from a Zippo lighter held by a stocky, brown-skinned woman in jeans and a denim shirt, her hair cut close to her scalp. She was crouched beside the lifeguard Angel had failed to protect; the man was slumped with his back to the wall. His eyes were glassy and a steel bar projected from the juncture of his shoulder and neck.

Angel drew closer. "Is he—"

"Still alive," the woman said. "Whatever they doped us with seems to have slowed down his metabolism. I've stopped the bleeding, but I can't take the bar out without starting it up again. I've got some medical training, but not enough to do surgery in a cave."

"'I'm Angel," he said, getting to one knee to take a closer look.

"Fisca. How come *you're* not drugged to the gills? When I first got here, I was sure I was back in Minneapolis at my grandmother's house. Could taste her oatmeal cookies and everything."

"I like to do things the old-fashioned way. I picked the severe-beating option instead."

She flashed a quick smile, but her eyes were frightened. "Why are we here? What do they want from us?"

"Is there anyone else here?" Angel asked.

"Yeah, there's a woman in the far corner. From her uniform, she's either a flight attendant or delivers strip-o-grams. Her nametag says Sarah. She's still out of it—kept babbling about summer camp and slumber parties. Lucky she finally shut up, or I would have strangled her."

"Better put out the light," Angel said. "Save it for when we need it."

Fisca closed the Zippo with a snap of her fingers, plunging them back into darkness.

"Don't worry," Angel said. "I'm going to get us—*all* of us—out of here."

He wished he felt as confident as he sounded.

Baasalt didn't know what to do.

Ever since the pick had been removed from his head, he'd been in a state of shock. He was operating purely on automatic now, going through the motions that were expected of him. He couldn't think of anything past the next few minutes.

All his ideas were gone.

No, that wasn't quite true. The ideas were still there, he could remember them all—but memories were all they were. They had been robbed of their vitality, their life. They were no longer *visions*.

Baasalt retreated to the alcove he called home. It was only a small, empty cave, since the Tremblors had virtually no possessions other than the occasional gemstone, admired for their geological perfection; he'd never been much for them himself. And spaciousness was a repellant concept, of course.

He considered retrieving the pickax from the Grounding Chamber. That would require explaining his actions to the council—and while an hour ago he would have had no problem doing so, now it seemed inconceivable. What would he say? How could he justify himself?

But he had to do *something*.

Wait. What if he sent someone else to fetch it?

He broadcast his thoughts. *Feldspaar. I require your assistance.*

Yes, Baasalt?

Go to the Grounding Chamber. Get the surface object I left there and bring it to me.

What shall I tell the Grounding?

Tell them I did not share my reasoning with you.

Baasalt—are you all right? Your thoughts have changed once more.

I'm fine. Do as I say!

Yes, First Warrior-Priest.

While he waited he closed his mind and meditated. After a short while he could feel the inquiring brush of the Grounding against his thoughts, but he chose to ignore it. He knew they would respect his privacy as First Warrior-Priest.

Eventually, Feldspaar came to his alcove. He had the pickax with him. Baasalt took it gratefully, then told Feldspaar to go. He needed to be alone.

He held the pickax in both hands, studying it. That such a simple thing could cause such changes . . . He ran a rough finger down the wooden handle, saw how the metal head was attached to it. He tapped a rocky claw against the tempered steel and listened to it ring.

Finally, reverently, he raised it to his head.

And found he couldn't quite reach the hole . . .

"Cindy! Cindy! Look what I've got!"

The voice came from the woman in the corner. "Oh, great," Fisca muttered. "Here we go again . . ."

Angel felt his way over to the corner in the dark. "Hello?" he said. He tried to remember the woman's name from the police report. "Sarah? Can you hear me?"

"Of course I can, silly. You're standing right there. Can you see *this*?"

"Uh—sure," Angel said. "What is it?"

"My mom's credit card—let's go shopping!"

"Sarah, listen to me. This isn't real. You have to try and concentrate—"

"Look, I'll study later, okay? I always do great at History, anyway. Come on, let's go to the mall."

Angel sighed. *Maybe if I play along I can get her to listen to me.* "All right," he said.

"Great! I know this *bitchin'* dress—it'll look great on you!"

"Uh—totally."

Angel shook his head in the dark. *It doesn't get much weirder than this . . .*

Stick it in my head, Baasalt told Feldspaar.

Once, Feldspaar would have questioned the wisdom of such an action. Now, he accepted the fact that Baasalt's wisdom was strange, new, and therefore unconventional. He did as he was instructed, sliding the point of the pickax back into the fissure it had previously made.

There was a jolt of neural energy, and Baasalt's mind was once more filled with exotic visions and ideas. His relieved happiness was so great that even Feldspaar could feel its effects.

Great Heart of the World, Feldspaar thought. *What wondrous joy . . .*

Yes. Yes! This is what I need—

Baasalt threw his arms wide and his head back in exultation.

The end of the pick struck the rock wall behind him. It drove the other end much deeper into Baasalt's brain.

The First Warrior-Priest's mind exploded.

"NOOOOOO!" Sarah screamed.

Angel, Fisca and the lifeguard screamed with her.

It felt like a hand-grenade going off at the base of Angel's skull. It felt like there was a giant finger-nail growing from the top of his head, and it was being scratched down an immense blackboard. It felt like every neuron he had detonated at the same time.

And not, he thought he heard Cordelia say, *in a good way.*

And then he was somewhere else.

Angel found himself in a shopping mall.

"Oookay," he said slowly. He looked around carefully.

It was not your everyday shopping mall. For one thing, the roof overhead was made of bare rock, sta-lactites hanging down like gray icicles. The people around him were behaving normally, but they were dressed in fashions from twenty years ago. Normally Angel didn't pay that much attention to fashion— two and a half centuries of trends had taught him that basic black was the easiest way to go—but these fashions were exaggerated, somehow; the col-lars seemed a little *too* wide, the ties a little *too* thin. There were a lot of neon colors: bright pink, lime-green, electric blue. Reality seen through a *Miami Vice* filter.

A teenaged version of Sarah was leaning against the wall beside him, rubbing her forehead. She was blond, pretty but gangly in that coltish way four-teen-year-old girls seemed to have trademarked.

"Wow, what a *rush,*" she said.

Angel glanced down at himself, half-expecting to find he'd been turned into a pubescent girl himself; thankfully, all he saw was his standard black trench-coat. "Sarah? Where are we?"

Sarah giggled. "We're at the mall, spaz. Come on—let's go shopping!" She grabbed his arm.

Angel let himself be led down the concourse. The stores were a strange mixture of the ordinary and the surreal: the dark mouths of caves were sand-wiched between clothing outlets and record stores.

"This can't be real," Angel said.

"Look!" Sarah said. "Shoes!" She dragged him into a shoe store.

There was a woman with long, dark hair standing in front of a wall of pumps. She turned at their approach.

"Hi, Angel!" Cordelia said brightly.

"Cordelia? What are you doing here?"

"You tell me—it's *your* subconscious." She looked down at herself, then up again. "Oh, and thanks for not imagining me naked. Or covered in blood."

"No problem," Angel answered. He glanced over at Sarah, who was busy trying on shoes. "My sub-conscious is a shoe store?"

Cordelia gave him a look. "Well, obviously it's not

just your subconscious, is it? I mean, *she's* here, isn't she?"

"Wait. Just before all this, something happened. Some kind of explosion that I felt in my brain . . ." Angel shook his head. "Why is it so hard to think?"

"Well, me boyo, y'must be tipsy, don't y'know?" said a familiar voice behind him.

Angel turned around. Doyle leaned against a wall, dressed in green jeans, green sneakers and a green T-shirt that read KISS ME I'M AN IRISH DEMON. He had a bottle of green whiskey with a big shamrock on the label in one hand. Little green horns jutted from his forehead. "A mind 'tis a wonderful thing to waste," Doyle said, and took a swig from the bottle. "Dependin' on whose mind it 'tis, o'course."

"Whose mind . . ." Angel muttered. "Not just mine. I'm in Sarah's mind, too. Something happened to link us together."

"Well, *duh*," Cordelia said.

"The Tremblors are telepathic," Angel said. He felt as if his mind were clearing a little. "This must be their doing."

"I'll drink t'that," Doyle said cheerfully, and did.

"The caves," Angel said. "If you two come from my subconscious and the mall from Sarah, the caves must represent the minds of the Tremblors."

"Whatever," Cordelia said with a shrug. She

picked up a pair of high heels and considered them. "Do you think these are too strappy?"

Angel walked out of the store, leaving Sarah, Doyle and Cordelia behind. None of them seemed to care except Doyle, who waved his whiskey bottle merrily in a good-bye.

Angel strode down the concourse, studying cave entrances as he went. They all looked pretty much the same—and then he saw something that stopped him dead.

The store was closed, its windows dark, a barred security gate across the door. Beyond the glass, Angel could make out the silhouettes of mannequins.

The sign over the door read ANGELUS FASHIONS.

Angel took a few steps closer. He could see a light on in the recesses of the shop. It flickered and seemed to grow stronger as he approached, like a candle when first lit.

He reached out, touched the bars of the gate. They were wrought iron, not the painted steel usually found in mall storefronts.

The gate unlocked with a loud click at his touch. It swung aside with a squeal of long-rusted hinges.

Angel paused with his hand on the doorknob. He knew he shouldn't go in, but he couldn't seem to stop himself. Something was pulling at him, drawing him closer. He couldn't resist it.

He opened the door and stepped inside.

Everything was covered in a fine layer of dust. His shoes left prints as distinct as if he were walking on the moon, grit crunching underfoot. A heavy velvet curtain in a red so deep it was almost black hung on one wall; an antique harpsichord stood in the corner. Wax dummies in frock coats and long gowns were posed here and there, their sculpted faces frozen in expressions of horror. They all looked familiar, and after a second Angel knew why. They were all people he'd killed.

The flickering light was coming from behind a thin cloth curtain that hung in a doorway beyond the front counter. Angel approached the counter, dread building in his heart. He knew he should turn around and run. He didn't.

Behind the curtain the light rose from waist- to chest-level. A lamp, being picked up. A hand appeared at the edge of the curtain and drew it aside.

Angelus grinned at him with a mouth full of curving fangs.

"Well, well, a customer, at long last. I was beginnin' t'think one would never show up . . . but you know what they say; in business, location is everything." His brogue, while not as exaggerated as Doyle's had been, gave a cheerful lilt to his voice.

Angel's mouth had gone dry. "You're not real," he said.

Angelus chuckled. He was wearing a black frock coat with a spray of white lace at the throat and cuffs, and held an oil lamp in one hand. "I'm as real as you are, Liam. Where d'you think I go when you're in charge and I'm not? I'm right here, locked away in your head. I see everything you see, hear everything you hear, know everything you know. Everything . . . and everyone."

Angelus hung the lamp from a hook beside the door, then came around the counter and stopped in front of Angel. "You might think I'm powerless, but I have more of an effect on you than you grasp. And caged though I am, I can afford t'be patient; I'm quite sure my time will come again."

Abruptly, the iron gate clanged shut.

"Why, my time might even be comin' up sooner than you'd expect. . . ."

CHAPTER ELEVEN

"Only one of us is walkin' out that door," Angelus said. "And it's not goin' t'be you."

Angel dropped into a fighting stance, but Angelus just laughed. "Think we're goin' t'settle this with fisticuffs, do you? If that's the way things worked, I would have been free long ago. No, no, my boy, this is a different sort of battlefield."

Angelus walked over to the nearest wax figure. It was a young woman in a peasant's simple dress, with a white bonnet and apron. Her eyes and mouth were open in terror. "Let's take a little stroll down memory lane . . . ah, sweet Annabelle. Do you remember her, Liam?"

"You know I do," Angel said grimly.

"Let's see just how well—" Angelus reached up and stroked the figure's cheek.

Wax became flesh. The woman's shriek was immediate and piercing. She sank to the floor, cowering and holding up her hands in self-defense. "Please," she sobbed. "Please, please, oh please . . ."

"That's enough," Angel snapped.

"That's not what you said back then," Angelus said with a smirk. "As a matter of fact, I believe it was three hours before you reached the point of 'enough.' But I really don't think it's necessary to go through the whole thing again—not when there are so many other lovely tidbits to sample."

"This isn't going to work," Angel said. "I didn't do these things. You did."

"Really? But you *remember* doing them, don't you? You remember the screams, the pleading, the things they offered if you'd only stop. The things they offered near the end were the sweetest, though, because they were the truest, the most heartfelt. And all they wanted at that point was simply to die. . . ."

"Stop it."

"You remember how it *smelled,* you remember how it *tasted*—and most of all, you remember how it felt. *You remember how much you enjoyed it.*"

"No," Angel whispered. Suddenly, his legs felt too weak to support him; he put a hand against the counter to steady himself.

"I apologize for the state of the shop, but it's hard

to keep up sometimes," Angelus said. He reached over to a velvet rope-pull hanging from the ceiling. "I know it doesn't look like much, but this is just the showroom; here, let me give you a look at the rest of my stock." He yanked on the rope, and the velvet curtain on the far side of the store drew aside.

The room it revealed was the size of a barn. Hundreds of wax figures stood, crouched or knelt in various poses; the expressions on their faces ranged from dawning fear to mindless horror.

"As you can see," Angelus said, "I have quite a collection to care for. Not that I'm complainin'; why, some of our finest moments are here."

Angel knew if he didn't leave in the next few moments, he never would. He could feel his strength leaving him.

"I've been thinkin' about that Gypsy curse," Angelus said. "It's what keeps me here, after all. But with you in here with me, I'm thinkin' the rules might be a little different. See, right now everythin's a little mixed up; the Tremblors, the sacrifice victims, you and me. Whatever happened, it's caught everybody's minds in the same net. Now, a simple Irish lad like myself doesn't know too much about mind-readin' and whatnot, but I do know this is a cell built for one, and all that really matters is that one of us stays. Since you were obligin' enough to waltz right in, I think there's a pretty fair chance I can waltz right out in your stead. Worth a try, wouldn't you say?"

"Never," Angel snarled, but there was a hint of desperation in it. Somehow, Angelus had gotten between him and the door.

Angelus stepped closer, until his face was inches away from Angel's own. "And d'you think you can stop me? I may be a prisoner, but after a hundred years I know my cage in a way you never will. It's full of things that give me strength and drain yours, and the longer you're here the weaker you become. That's your fatal flaw, you see—you burden yourself with useless guilt. Whereas I—"

He grabbed the front of Angel's trenchcoat with both hands. "I feel only simple satisfaction."

He launched Angel up and backward with one convulsive two-handed thrust, sending him flying over the tops of the still figures to land sprawling in the middle of them.

Angel was back on his feet in an instant, but before he could do anything else, Angelus clapped his hands together.

All the figures surrounding Angel were suddenly alive.

Angel knew that was impossible. After all, he could clearly remember murdering each and every one . . .

Angelus laughed, and headed for the door.

When the steel pickax plunged into Baasalt's brain, it penetrated the telepathic center in his cerebral cortex. The immense jolt his mind received was broadcast to every other Tremblor.

Most of them, unused to abrupt sensory input, went into shock. They tried to retreat into their own minds in self-defense, and were unable to. Some were actually stunned by the sheer mental impact.

And at the center of the psychic maelstrom, the First Warrior-Priest was having another epiphany.

It was unlike the previous bursts of insight he'd experienced. Rather than an explosion of ideas and concepts, Baasalt felt *himself* expand. His mind spread itself through the psychic web every Tremblor was part of, though they rarely used telepathy for group communication; more than three or four minds speaking together became a chaotic jumble that was hard to make out. The Grounding sometimes made pronouncements to all the Tremblors at once, and there were mental tournaments every few centuries, but proclamations were strictly one-way, and the tournaments had rigidly defined rules.

Baasalt was in simultaneous contact with every member of his race. Even through their shock and fear, he felt that each Tremblor was part of him, and that together, they were unstoppable.

That conviction slowly seeped into the minds of his

people. It calmed them, gave them something to focus on. The source of the storm now became its savior.

Their savior.

His hand was on the doorknob when something struck Angelus in the back. It propelled him forward, smashing his face through the glass door and into the steel bars of the gate on the other side. An instant later he was yanked backward, falling to the floor amid shards of glass.

He looked up into Angel's grim face. "Little tip," Angel said. "When you send an army of the dead to run interference for you, don't pick people who are terrified of your target."

Angelus glanced at the room of victims. They were all cowering in the corners, gibbering in fear. "Ah, well," he said cheerfully. "I prefer the old-fashioned approach, anyway."

He launched himself at Angel, slamming his shoulder into Angel's stomach and driving him backward into the counter. Angel responded with a knee to his foe's belly, then grabbed him by the hair and smashed his head into the counter—once, twice, three times.

Angelus broke his hold and delivered a round-house to Angel's jaw. Angel staggered back, parried the next punch and threw one of his own.

They went at it, toe-to-toe. Kick, punch, block.

Punch, block, kick. It went on and on, the shop fading away into a gray oblivion around them as their universe contracted to a purely personal one of attack and retaliation.

They were too perfectly matched, Angel realized. It was a fight that could go on forever, unless something changed. From the look on his enemy's face, he could tell he'd reached the same conclusion.

"Well, this has been fun," Angelus said as they grappled, "and don't think I haven't dreamed of beating your brains in for the past century, but I believe our dance is up." He broke away from Angel abruptly, and the confines of the shop snapped back into focus. "Time for a little somethin' I was keepin' in reserve."

"There's nothing you can throw at me I can't handle," Angel growled.

"No? There's a bit of history that's been gnawin' at you lately, my boy. I think it might be just enough t'tip the scales. C'mon out, darlin'!"

And from out of the doorway Angelus had appeared from stepped Maria. She looked just like the last time Angel had seen her, in the ruins of a church cellar in 1755.

"No," Angel whispered.

Yes. The thought was that of every Tremblor, united in a single purpose. That purpose was the will of the First Warrior-Priest.

No. A single cry of dissent; not every Tremblor, then. Baasalt turned his attention to the one who opposed him, and discovered that it was six minds, speaking as one. The Grounding.

Join us, Baasalt thought. *Join us and I will lead our race to greatness.*

No. The thought was firm. *This unity is an illusion. You impose your wishes upon minds weaker than your own.*

Those minds are stronger, now. I add my strength, my vision, to theirs. Our wishes are the same.

Your wishes are madness. We were willing to overlook your eccentricities until you had fulfilled your duties in the Crushing of Souls—but now we see we can wait no longer.

Baasalt could feel something building in the minds of the Grounding, a concentration of mental energy. *What are you doing?* he demanded.

Restoring the balance.

Maria was not alone, of course. There was also the dead body she was lashed to, face-to-face.

She shuffled forward in a horrible parody of a waltz, his limbs moving with hers. Angelus had stripped off their clothing before tying them together, limb to limb, torso to torso, so she would feel his dead, naked flesh against every inch of her own. He had broken all her fingers to prevent her from untying the knots, and rigged a hangman's noose around a beam and the corpse's neck to keep them upright. The rope trailed down the corpse's back like a necktie thrown over the shoulder of a drunken executive.

She staggered forward, trying to form words with bloody lips. She couldn't, of course; he had ripped her tongue out so she couldn't cry for help.

"Some of your *best* work," Angelus said. "And you didn't even kill her, just lit some candles and then sealed the place back up. Left her there, swaying slowly back and forth with her silent partner, staring into his blank eyes as the candles burned down. Your last words echoing in her ears, as you showed her how clever you'd been with the rope; how all it would take to undo the whole thing and free herself was to release the loop around his neck. Of course, the rope was far too tough to gnaw through, and she'd be long dead of thirst or hunger by the time his head rotted off—which left her one very unpleasant choice. She could die in the dark, bound to a dead man, or she could lean forward and take that first, fleshy bite—"

"I remember," Angel said tonelessly. He felt like every muscle in his body had seized up. In another second, Angelus would bolt for the door, and he wouldn't be able to stop him . . .

"Hey, is this place, like, open?" Sarah said from the doorway.

Angel reacted without thinking, and it saved them both. He shoved Maria into Angelus and dove for Sarah. His momentum carried both of them out of the shop, and the door clanged shut behind them.

"What's your *damage*?" Sarah said crossly.

"At the moment, mainly self-loathing. . . ."

Power surged from the Grounding, a mental attack directed at Baasalt himself. Lightning crackled in his skull, thunderbolts spiking agony into his brain, then arcing throughout the psychic web Baasalt had established. It shattered under the blow.

Baasalt found himself alone once more. *No,* he thought. *NO!* He reached out, seeking that all-encompassing connection once more.

He was rejected. The Tremblors had reached their limit for the new and the strange; after the lightning bolt of pain each of them had felt, they wanted nothing more to do with the First Warrior-Priest.

The same could not be said for the Grounding.

You will answer for your actions, the Batholith thought.

We will see, answered Baasalt. He closed his mind to further messages.

Baasalt? Feldspaar thought. Baasalt stalked out of his alcove and past his former comrade without replying. He was First Warrior-Priest no longer, he knew.

Now, he was a heretic—and a fugitive.

There was a flash in his head, and Angel found himself back in his rocky cell.

At least Angel assumed that's where he was; he was in total darkness again. A second later and Fisca's Zippo flared, confirming the situation.

"Whoa," Fisca said in a shaky voice. "What was all *that* about?"

"It affected you, too?" Angel asked. "What did you see?"

"I was on the bottom floor of some kind of mall. All the stores seemed to have something to do with my life—there was even a place having a sale on all the clothes I've ever worn, stuff from when I was a kid right up to my latest sports bra. It was *bizarre*."

"Tell me about it," Angel muttered.

"Ohhh," Sarah groaned. "What—where am I? What's going on?"

"Looks like she's coming out of it," Fisca said. "The other guy's still zonked."

"Sarah?" Angel said. "You're among friends. Listen to me very carefully. . . ." Angel explained as best he could, making the Tremblors sound like a cult that dressed up in strange costumes and drugged their victims.

When he was done, Sarah said, "What are they going to do with us?"

"Nothing," Angel said flatly. "I won't let them, and I have associates who know what's happened to me. Don't worry, help is on its way . . ."

You've captured the vampire? Associate Rome thought. *What a pleasant surprise.*

I thought you might be pleased, Baasalt responded. *Our previous contacts gave me the impression you and he have clashed before.*

Not directly. However, his interests are generally at odds with my employers. They would be most pleased if I could provide evidence of his demise.

Perhaps you would like to attend the ritual?

The Crushing of Souls? I didn't think outsiders were allowed.

I am First Warrior-Priest. I am sure I can convince the Grounding to make an exception, but I would require a favor in return.

When Baasalt told him what he needed, Rome chuckled to himself, then agreed to supply what Baasalt had asked for.

Baasalt had a plan.

After leaving the Tremblors, he had tunneled to a

spot much closer to the Skin of the World, collapsing the tunnel behind him. He did not think the Grounding would send anyone after him, but he wanted to ensure his privacy.

Normally, the Tremblors were spread throughout the Body of the World; over the last year, they had slowly been gathering under L.A. The Crushing of Souls was one of the few times all the Tremblors would come together physically, in the presence of the Grounding. That was when he would strike.

He couldn't risk contacting any of the other warrior-priests beforehand; when the moment came, he would have to gamble that enough would stand with him to let him act. He was reasonably sure Feldspaar and Maarl would be among his allies—but far from certain.

Alone in self-imposed exile, he shivered with the delicious, chaotic, *unpredictability* of it all . . .

"Do you really think this'll work?" Galvin asked.

"It's gotta," Doyle answered.

They stood in Galvin's apartment. All the wrecked furniture and art had been removed; it was now a staging area for an invasion. Lumber for shoring up tunnels was stacked against one wall, while shovels, buckets and mining helmets were still being unpacked. The tunnel entrance the Tremblors had made was now brightly illuminated as busy Serpentene rigged lights and ventilation.

"Wow," Cordelia said, pulling clothing from a crate. "I didn't know Armani *made* industrial coveralls."

"What about the other thing?" Doyle asked nervously.

"It's on its way," Galvin assured him. "I hope we can get it down the tunnel, but you seem to know what you're doing."

"Oh, I'm practically an expert," Doyle said. "I've seen *The Great Escape* five times."

"Hopefully, we won't have to do too much actual digging," Galvin said. "If your reasoning holds, the Tremblors will only have collapsed short lengths of their tunnels, making it easier if they decide to return."

"And preparation for their ritual should keep 'em too occupied to post guards," Doyle added. "I don't think they'll be expectin' us t'take the fight to their turf."

"I don't know about this, Galvin," Maureen said, stepping over to his side. "We're not soldiers. What if it doesn't work? What if they decide to retaliate? What if—what if—" She was close to tears.

"We have to do something," Galvin said softly. He put a hand on Maureen's shoulder. "As it stands, they think they can attack us anytime they want. We have to show them they're wrong; not out of pride or anger, but as a simple matter of survival. Come on, Maureen—you're a tough negotiator, you know how this works. We don't show some backbone now, they'll eat us for breakfast."

Maureen gave him a shaky smile and wiped her eyes. "I know, I know. But it's hard to be strong when all I can think of is the kids."

"Hang in there," Cordelia said. "We've still got Angel, too. Prisoner or not, he'll come through. He always does. Why, I bet he's cooking up a brilliantly violent escape plan right now . . ."

"Got any threes?" Angel asked.

"Go fish," said Fisca.

Angel sighed. "You know, this would be a lot easier if we had cards."

"What for? We couldn't see 'em anyway. And it was your idea in the first place."

"They haven't fed us. That's a bad sign," Sarah said. Her voice was calm, almost detached. "It's one of the things they taught us at flight school. In a hostage situation, if they don't feed you it's because they're planning to kill you."

"Just take it easy," Angel said. "Nobody's getting killed."

"Don't patronize me," Sarah said. "I'm not hysterical, I'm not in shock. I may not be a paratrooper, but I've been trained to handle myself under stress. This definitely qualifies."

"I'm sorry," Angel said. "I wasn't sure how you were handling things. The last time we talked you thought I was a fourteen-year-old girl."

"How's our other friend?" Sarah asked.

"Still breathing," Fisca said. "He needs a doctor, though—and soon."

Rome waited for Baasalt in a sewer. He was dressed in top-of-the-line mountaineering gear, from his Gore-Tex jacket to his expensive hiking boots. He sat on top of a waterproof crate, his bony frame perched like some kind of underground stork. He smoked a cigarette and watched the dirty water swirl past.

The curving cement wall twenty feet away began to hum, then to vibrate. It exploded outward in a shower of concrete chunks.

Baasalt appeared in the new opening. *Rome. You have brought what I requested?*

"It's right here," Rome said, patting the crate.

The Tremblor stalked forward, splashing through the water and stopping in front of Rome. The thin man hopped off the crate, leaned over it and popped the latch, showing the Quake demon what he'd brought.

Baasalt studied the contents quietly. *Good*, he

thought at last. He closed the crate, relatched it and then picked it up, tucking it under one massive arm. *Come with me.*

Baasalt returned to the opening he'd made. Associate Rome followed.

They'd tried, over and over, to come up with a plan. The best they could do was demand medical help on the pretext that the lifeguard was about to die; Angel was pretty sure the Tremblors needed him alive for the ceremony. But an hour of yelling had gotten them nothing but sore throats, and the boulder the entrance was blocked with was too large for even Angel to move.

So now they sat in the dark, each one alone with his or her thoughts. Their voices were too hoarse for casual conversation.

Angel's thoughts kept turning to Maria.

Angel had wished, more than once, that he could separate himself completely from the actions of Angelus. That he could say *this is me and what I've done* and *that was him, that was all his doing.* But he couldn't, because it wasn't true. He remembered *being* Angelus, he remembered every detail with crystal clarity.

Worst of all, he remembered how much he'd liked it.

Just like Angelus said.

And what he'd done to Maria . . . he'd actually been proud of that. Darla had called him a genius. They had entertained themselves more than once by trying to guess which choice Maria had finally made, whether she'd tried to gnaw her way free or had simply given up and waited to die, waited for her thirst and hunger to grow. Waited for the rats.

And whether the choice she'd made had driven her mad.

He'd never gone back to check. Other diversions kept him entertained. For all he knew, she'd survived, grown stronger as a result of her ordeal and gone on to have a long life.

Sometimes he almost believed that. Now was not one of those times.

For a hundred years he'd punished himself, retreating into a lonely, filthy existence. The only thing that had kept him from suicide was the guilt itself; death would be an escape, and he deserved to suffer.

That old black pit of despair still yawned beneath him, making him feel like he lived on a tightrope stretched across it—but he'd found something that gave him balance.

He helped others now. While that also added to his burden, it gave him a reason to go on, to refuse to dive off that tightrope. Part of Angel truly believed he belonged sealed in a cave in the bowels of the Earth—but it was countered by the belief that Sarah, Fisca and the lifeguard did not.

They would not die, alone in the dark. They would not have to make one final, terrible choice.

Even if Angel had to die in their place.

Associate Rome followed Baasalt for the better part of an hour, a Mag-lite discreetly pointed downward to ensure his footing.

I'm surprised you accepted my offer, Baasalt thought.

"I have very good reasons for doing so," Rome answered aloud in his gravelly voice. "The vampire has interfered in our firm's business before. The senior partners would view someone who could eliminate that interference in a very favorable light."

You are not the one doing the eliminating, Baasalt pointed out.

"Perhaps not directly . . . but ultimately, I am responsible. Most importantly, I am the one who will bring confirmation of the vampire's demise. In my world, a messenger bringing bad news is sometimes blamed for the news itself—and I can assure you, the opposite principle applies."

Ah. I believe I understand. News is information leading to change. My people also have strong feelings about this concept.

"And how do they tend to react?"

That is yet to be decided.

Baasalt suddenly stopped. His body language suggested he was listening, but Rome heard nothing. If he were communicating with his people, it was at a frequency Rome couldn't receive.

"Baasalt?" he prompted.

Baasalt held up a hand, signaling Rome to wait.

After a full minute, Baasalt began to move forward again. His thoughts were strangely silent.

Angel jumped to his feet when he heard the sound of the boulder being moved aside. A second later, a thin beam of light shone through the crack.

"Who's there?" Angel asked.

"My name is Rome," a voice rasped. "I doubt if you know who I am."

Angel sniffed the air. "Maybe not, but I recognize the smell. Lawyer, with a hint of brimstone. I'd say you work for Wolfram and Hart."

Rome chuckled throatily. "Very good—but then, that *is* your profession. Or at least it was."

"Wolfram and Hart?" Sarah gasped. "But—but they're who represented me last year."

"That they did, Miss Clark. Have you forgotten our arrangement?"

"*What* arrangement?" Sarah demanded. "My

lawyer said something about my being a possible future asset, but I thought—oh."

"You thought we meant to utilize your abilities as a smuggler," Rome said. He coughed. "Excuse me—rock dust." He cleared his throat, then continued. "You thought that since we so cleverly got you acquitted—when you were undeniably in possession of a large quantity of cocaine—that we would require your services in a similar capacity. Sadly, that is not the case."

"I know this bloodsucker," Fisca growled. The light shifted to her face, making her blink.

"Hello, Louise," Rome said. "Yes, I remember you, as well. One doesn't quickly forget a woman who burned her ex-lover to death. Actually, you're the only one I've met before; the rest of you I got from our files."

The light shifted again, coming to rest on the slack face of the lifeguard. "I see Mr. Norden isn't doing so well. If he regains consciousness before he dies, ask him if he's gotten over that nasty little serial-rape problem of his."

There was a moment of strained silence.

"Why are you here?" Angel said. "You come all this way just to gloat?"

"Yes."

"Oh."

"Actually, I came down to tell you the details of

my evil scheme, Angel—all the pieces of the puzzle you haven't quite figured out. The reason for all this intrigue, the machinations behind the scenes, all the hard work I've put in with nobody to appreciate my brilliance. Nobody, of course, but my noble adversary. And now that you're about to die, I see no reason not to share my—excuse me—my plans—" He began to cough, then hawked and spat.

"This dust is really getting to my throat," he said. "You know, never mind. Have a nice death."

The boulder slid back into place, cutting off the beam of light.

"I don't think I like that guy," Angel said.

CHAPTER TWELVE

$What$ was the $point$ of $that?$ Baasalt thought as they walked away.

"I despise the self-righteous. I want him to go to his death wondering if it was all worthwhile, or if he's thrown his life away trying to help those that didn't deserve it. I want him to agonize over his choices. . . ."

They had gone no more than a dozen paces when two Tremblors appeared from a side passage. This time, the volume of their thoughts was perceptible to Rome.

Baasalt. The Grounding requires your presence.

Of course. I was just on my way to see them.

Why is a Skin-Dweller with you?

That is a question I will answer when the Grounding asks it.

Very well.

The Tremblors took up positions on either side of Rome and Baasalt. The four of them continued onward.

At length they came to the chamber of the Grounding. The pool of lava in the middle of the six columns of rock glowed a hellish orange-red and made the air in the room shimmer with heat waves.

The two Tremblors that accompanied them took up positions at the mouth of the tunnel. Rome and Baasalt approached the first and largest of the columns. Baasalt put down the crate he was carrying at the foot of the column.

Great Batholith, he began. *I am here to beg forgiveness.*

Forgiveness? Is that why you have brought a Skin-Dweller here, to our most sacred place?

This is no ordinary Skin-Dweller. He is a representative of our allies on the Skin of the World, the one who made it possible to obtain the Four.

We see. And the reason for his presence?

He simply wishes to observe. One of the Four is his enemy, and witnessing his destruction will give him great pleasure.

You are in no position to ask for favors, Baasalt. You have much to answer for.

I have the answers you require right here. Baasalt knelt and opened the crate.

Inside, packed end-to-end, were six stainless-steel pickaxes.

Baasalt picked one up, hefted it. *I had planned to do this during the ceremony itself,* Baasalt thought. *But I see now I was merely bowing to tradition.* He moved suddenly behind the Batholith.

Before either of the Tremblors at the entrance could move, Baasalt swung, sinking the pickax into the Batholith's brain.

Rome felt the surge of psychic energy, but he'd taken the precaution of having a warding spell performed before he left the surface; his mind was unaffected.

The other Tremblors were not so lucky.

The minds of the Grounding were the oldest and most powerful of all their race, and the Batholith was the strongest of all. If he'd had time, he could have frozen Baasalt with a thought; but Baasalt had done something the Grounding would never have suspected a Tremblor capable of. He had acted impulsively.

The mental backlash arced from the Batholith to the rest of the Grounding, then to Baasalt, then to all the other Tremblors. The Grounding did their best to suppress it, but the effort of battling their most powerful member left them weak and dazed.

Baasalt felt only invigorated. This was his fourth exposure to such a mental rush, and he welcomed it.

Leaving the pick embedded, he grabbed another from the crate. He approached the next column.

"Well," Rome said. "This certainly isn't what I expected . . ."

The Tremblors weren't the only ones affected.

The previous mindstorm that flooded through the brains of the captives had poured through Sarah first, her psychic defenses being lowest. Her perceptions had colored theirs, giving rise to the mall scenario.

This time, it was different.

It was Baasalt's mind that focused the psychic torrent. It was Baasalt's vision they suddenly found themselves living in.

Thick, choking clouds of volcanic ash swirled around them. A blood-red sun shone dimly above. It took Angel a second to realize they were standing in the middle of a city street, the pavement cracked and dusty. Parked vehicles on the side of the road were almost unidentifiable under a thick layer of ash, and the buildings that rose beyond them were only hazy mountains. The air was hot, dry, and thick; Sarah and Fisca immediately started coughing.

"What *is* this place?" Sarah choked out.

Before Angel could answer, a loud *KLANG!* reverberated through their heads. They didn't so much hear it as feel it, as if their bones had become tuning forks. It sounded like the death knell of a god.

And the ground began to rumble.

"Earthquake!" Fisca yelled. There was no chance to run, and nowhere to run to. The earth moved beneath them like a runaway elevator, throwing them all to the ground. There was a sickeningly *wrong* feeling to the movement, as if some natural law had just been broken.

The air filled with the death-screams of dying skyscrapers: the screeching, rending noise of over-stressed metal, punctuated by staccato bursts of shattering windows. Razored shards of glass dropped out of the sky in a deadly rain.

KLAAANG! Again, the ominous sound reverberated through them—and again, everything changed.

Angel was in a line of men and women, slowly shuffling forward, all dressed in filthy rags. They were in a narrow stone corridor, moving toward an open doorway outlined in flickering light. As Angel drew closer, he saw that people who reached the doorway weren't so much stepping through it as falling.

When he reached the doorway, he saw why. It opened onto a deep underground pit, with a pool of red-hot lava waiting far below. There were three other doorways spaced around the perimeter across from him; he saw three other haunted faces that had reached the end of their lines.

And then the line moved forward, and all of them were falling.

KLAAANG!

Angel shook his head, disoriented. Where was he now?

The same thick clouds of dust hung in the air, obscuring visibility. Angel looked down and saw neatly trimmed, even green grass between his feet. He was in a park—or on a playing field.

"Sarah? Fisca?" he called out.

"Over here!" Fisca's voice—followed a second later by a meaty *thump!* and a shriek of pain. Angel broke into a run, heading for the sound.

The first rock caught Angel square between the shoulder blades, turning his run into a headlong plunge into the turf. He had barely scrambled to his feet when the next one hit, glancing off his shoulder and knocking him down again.

"Stop it!" screamed Sarah, somewhere to his left. "Stop it, just *stop it!*"

The dull *thud* of rocks came all around him now. He heard a few crunches, too.

This isn't real, Angel thought. He closed his eyes and tried to shut it all out.

KLANNNGG!

Angel opened his eyes.

What he saw didn't make sense at first. Gradually he realized that what he was seeing was part dream, part plan. It was a Tremblor's-eye view of the entire planet.

It was a labyrinth that went on forever. Tunnels that not just honeycombed the planet but erupted from the surface in huge earthen pipes that snaked their way across the landscape, through the ruins of cities that had been shaken apart by multiple quakes. Hundreds of volcanoes spewed molten rock into the air, blanketing the Earth in a cloud of ash, choking the rivers and turning the ocean to sludge. Tremblors stalked the land unafraid, and humans were kept like cattle.

The visions had grown stronger with each succeeding toll of the unseen bell, and this latest one was the strongest of all. It came with an emotional flavor, one that Angel recognized. It was the pure, heady taste of obsession, bringing with it a clarity of purpose that erased all doubts, all fears, and replaced them with a fierce joy.

It was a taste Angel had known all too well. It was the secret drug he was ashamed to admit he sometimes still craved, and as that joy tried to impose itself on his soul, he felt the Angelus inside him welcome it with open arms. Welcome it as he began to rise to the surface . . .

"NO!" Angel rejected the imagery with every ounce of his will.

It was enough to snap him free; there was no

place in the shared mind for dissension. There was only a single, terrible sense of purpose, and Angel felt it recede from him as if he were falling from a burning aircraft.

He was in his cell once more. Fisca and Sarah had joined the lifeguard in unconsciousness; that, or they were still trapped in the Tremblor's vision of certainty.

Angel was certain of only two things: first, that the Quake demons were now unified in a new and terrifying way.

Second, they were now all insane.

"He'll be all right," Doyle said. "Angel's a pro." His group was taking a break topside, while another team of five Serpentene kept digging. Buckets of dirt were emptied into side passages, of which there were quite a few. Doyle just hoped they were on the right course.

"Sure," Cordelia said. "I mean, two of the things generally in short supply in underground caves are sunlight and wooden stakes, right? So down there he'll practically be Superman."

"Well, there is the matter of lava," Doyle said.

"What? Nobody mentioned lava! What does lava have to do with anything?" Cordelia demanded, pacing back and forth. "These are supposed to be earthquake demons, not—not Hawaiian volcano demons! And Angel's not even a virgin!"

Maureen handed her a glass of Scotch and led her to a chair. "Just take it easy," she said. "We're working as hard as we can."

Cordelia sat, then gulped her drink. "I know, I know. I just wish I could do something useful."

"Well, you could help dig," Doyle said.

"Doyle, I'm trying to be serious," Cordelia said.

"Sorry."

"Perhaps I can cheer you up a bit," Galvin said, emerging from the mouth of the tunnel. He'd been supervising their progress, organizing the work details and arranging for supplies. "I understand you had a bit of trouble at the office. Well, I think that comes under the heading of expenses, which makes it my responsibility." He fished in the pocket of his overalls and pulled out a check. "I had someone go over there and do an estimate on repairs. I know it's cold comfort, but at least it's one less thing to worry about." He handed the check to Cordelia.

"Thanks, Galvin," Cordelia said. She tucked the check into her pocket without even looking at it.

Now Doyle knew just how worried she was.

Angel was truly on his own now.

He used Fisca's Zippo to take inventory. He made a decision.

First, he took apart one of his wrist harnesses. He removed the short, hollow metal tube that a

275

wooden stake was usually seated in and examined it critically.

He took it over to where the lifeguard sat slumped against the rocky wall, breathing shallowly. He tried to fit the hollow tube over the steel bar, but it didn't quite fit. Angel spent the next few minutes using a small rock and his own strength to crimp the tube into a more square shape.

Finally, he was able to slide the tube over the bar. He took the modified tube and used Fisca's keys like tongs to hold it over the flame of the Zippo. He got it as hot as he could, then slid it over the metal bar like a sheath.

"Sorry about this," Angel said to the comatose lifeguard. He used the keys to slide the heated tube down the bar, and into the wound itself.

The stink of burning flesh was immediate. Angel held his breath, hoping the heated metal would both sterilize and cauterize the puncture, preventing infection and bleeding. The squared tube was barely long enough to reach all the way through the wound.

Holding the tube in place with the keys, Angel slowly pulled the bar out.

It worked. The tube plugged the hole, there didn't seem to be any additional bleeding and the lifeguard never twitched. Angel had a weapon.

The bar was almost two feet in length, longer

than the stakes he usually used. Angel was pretty sure he could modify his two wrist harnesses into one that held the bar, letting him conceal it up his sleeve.

He got to work.

"I think I'm through," Doyle said.

He dug faster, clearing dirt away from the growing opening. The other members of his crew shone lights through, revealing another long, dark tunnel. It seemed unoccupied.

"Well, what do you think?" Ian said.

And then the rumbling began.

"Oh, *shite*," Doyle said.

A tremor shook the ground, knocking both of them off their feet, while dirt rained down from above. Doyle huddled against a wooden support, waiting for it to come crashing down.

Angel felt the tremors, too, but he ignored them. He was preparing himself.

The Zippo had run out of fuel, forcing him to complete the last of the harness modifications in the dark. He'd worked by touch, taking his time, being as deliberate and thorough as he could. A mistake now could prove fatal later.

He was done. All that was left was to wait.

He sat cross-legged, his hands open at his sides.

He cleared his mind. The tremors that shook the earth did not matter. The smell of blood from the lifeguard's wounds did not matter. The gnawing thirst in his throat, his stomach, did not matter.

All that mattered was to be ready.

The rumbling stopped. Doyle realized he wasn't dead; the tunnel supports had held.

A few moments later the thick dust was cut by the beams of the returning Serpentene, who'd run up the tunnel when the quake had started. They called Doyle and Ian's name, and Doyle managed to cough out an answer. Ian didn't. He'd been struck by a falling rock and was out cold.

They hauled both of them out, dressed Ian's scalp wound and poured each a medicinal shot of brandy. Since Ian was still unconscious, Doyle drank his, too.

"How bad is it?" Galvin asked.

"Hard t'say. Our section held, but I don't know how much came down."

"So what do we do?" Cordelia asked.

"We keep diggin'," Doyle said. "And hope we didn't just use up the last of our luck."

Baasalt surveyed the results of his handiwork.

The six stone columns that comprised the Grounding now each sported a pickax. Two of the members no longer seemed to be functioning, but that did not concern Baasalt. What were two among many—especially when the many were one?

He turned his attention inward, to the newfound unity he'd forged. All the Tremblor minds were as a single being now, an extension of his own will. His thoughts ran through their minds, and theirs through his. But while their minds had been predictable and rigid, his was the rushing torrent of an underground river, the unrelenting white-hot flow of molten rock. He had created his own ritual, sacrificing his tribe's individuality to shape a new being.

But creating new traditions didn't mean forgetting about old ones. Oh, no. The Crushing of Souls would go forward as planned—but with the vampire's soul as the Fourth Sacrifice, the race Baasalt would bring forth would be greater than any that had gone before. A race of conquerors, a race composed entirely of Warrior-Priests. They would transform the World, from its Heart to its Skin, and Baasalt would be their leader.

Come, he thought. *Come, my children. It is time to gather for the birth of something new.*

It is time for the Crushing of Souls.

It is time for the Dance of the Sleeping Giants.

And in their alcoves, in their caves and tunnels and hidden places in the earth, the Tremblors stirred and began to move. One by one, they converged on what had been the chamber of the Grounding, and the pool of magma that glowed in its center.

When they came for him, Angel went peacefully.

They marched him down a tunnel, two Tremblors in front of him and two behind. Three other Quake demons carried the still-comatose bodies of the others.

Angel kept his right arm stiff by his side; the steel bar up his sleeve kept him from bending his elbow. He'd be fine as long as no one asked to shake hands. Somehow, he doubted that would come up.

After a ten-minute hike, he found himself back in the chamber of the Grounding. There had been some changes: the pool of magma seemed fuller than the last time he was there, the temperature had gone from winter in Miami to summer in Death Valley . . . and all six columns of stone now had steel pickaxes embedded in them.

That, and the place was filled with Quake demons.

They stood in a circle around the perimeter of the chamber. Waves of heat rising from the lava pit made the air shimmer. Angel did a quick estimate, and came up with around two hundred; probably the whole tribe, from what his research had indicated. They were still as statues, not even moving their heads to look at Angel and his entourage when they arrived—with two exceptions.

Associate Rome stood beside one of the columns, drinking a bottle of Perrier. He wiped his brow with a white handkerchief, then waved as if they were two members of a country club running into each other on the golf course.

"Don't mind me," he said. "You won't even know I'm here."

A Tremblor with a pickax protruding from the back of his head nodded at Angel. He stood in the narrow ring between the edge of the lava pit and the six stone columns, which is where the Tremblors laid the limp forms of Fisca, Sarah and the lifeguard, spacing them evenly around the pit.

Angel himself was brought face-to-face with Baasalt.

It is fitting that you face your death with your mind intact, Baasalt thought.

"Wish I could say the same about you," Angel answered. "I think you've made a horrible mistake in your interpretation of the phrase 'I'd like to pick your brain.' "

What you Skin-Dwellers call humor, correct? A strange reaction in the face of imminent destruction; I shall have to study it, once I have bent the surface world to my will. So much to learn . . .

"Well, I've been told I'm a helluva teacher. My lessons tend to stick for the rest of my pupils' lives—usually a good two or three seconds. Five, tops."

Then consider this to be my lesson to you.

Baasalt reached out and wrapped one rocky claw around Angel's throat.

Angel tensed, but didn't move. He felt the Tremblor trying to invade his mind; normally that was impossible with a vampire, but Baasalt's mind seemed different, and if the Quake demon sensed his plan, Angel wouldn't have a chance. Angel forced his mind to be still, to be calm, to be blank . . .

To be a void.

Baasalt's probe recoiled suddenly. Angel's mind unsettled him in a deeply conditioned way; as much as all Tremblors loathed large, empty spaces, they were completely unused to encountering such a thing on a mental level. Baasalt withdrew, disturbed but still confident.

It was time.

Fellow Tremblors. All of you know the First Story, of how the Ig explored the Body of the World . . .

Angel recognized the cadence of a ritual begun. He knew the Tremblors' concentration would be focused, that the outside world would mean less and less as the ritual progressed. He also knew the ritual involved him and the other three being tossed into the pit of lava, but he didn't know exactly *when*.

He had to act now.

Baasalt's claw was still wrapped around his throat. The Quake demon could crush Angel's windpipe simply by closing his fist—which meant the first order of business was getting him to let go.

Angel focused his own concentration. The Tremblors were made of rock and were inhumanly strong, but they still walked on two feet, had arms and legs and hands. From an engineering standpoint, they had many of the same weak spots a human being had; they were simply better armored.

All armor has flaws, Angel thought. *All mountains have fissures.*

All arms have elbows.

Two feet of tempered steel dropped into his right hand at the flick of a wrist. He crossed his left hand over to join his right in a *katana*-style grip, and drove the point of the bar sideways into the elbow joint of Baasalt's arm as hard as he could.

The joint snapped, sounding like a sledgehammer cracking granite. The Tremblor lost his grip on Angel as his arm suddenly bent the wrong way.

Angel dropped to a crouch, drew back his

weapon and lunged forward again. This time, he went for Baasalt's knee.

Another loud crack, and Angel was rolling out of the way as Baasalt crashed to the ground. He wound up at the foot of Associate Rome, who tried to punt him over the lip of the pit.

Angel dodged the kick and leapt to his feet. Rome immediately stepped back, not interested in a fair fight.

As much as Angel wanted to protect the other captives, he simply couldn't do it at the moment. They were too spread out, in hard-to-defend positions. The best he could do was hold his own ground, and hope they couldn't continue the ritual without him.

He backed his way into a small alcove. It was barely more than an indent in the wall of the cave, but it was made of solid rock from floor to ceiling; the Tremblors wouldn't be able to burrow in from behind or underneath him as easily as they could through dirt. At the very least, he'd be able to hear them coming.

No, the only way to attack him now was one-on-one—the opening was too narrow to admit more than a single Quake demon at a time.

The first Tremblor rushed forward. Angel rammed the end of the steel bar into the Quake demon's throat, bringing him to a halt, then kicked him in the chest and sent him sprawling.

Angel summoned his vampire side, his face distorting into a yellow-eyed mask of fury. "Who's next?" he snarled.

Another one rushed him. Angel beat him back with a vicious series of strikes to the eyes and neck. The demon withdrew in pain.

"You're just delaying the inevitable," Rome called out.

"Oh, I don't know. I'm kind of having fun."

You will tire, long before we do, Baasalt thought.

"Think so? I'll tell you what I think. I think if I do enough damage to your troops, they're going to start to doubt you. And once that happens, you're finished. That's the flip side of being a dictator, Baasalt—total control means total responsibility. Something goes wrong, you're the first one to get blamed."

Then I shall have to ensure nothing goes wrong.

The crowd of Tremblors at the mouth of the alcove suddenly parted. Baasalt stood about twenty feet away, beside one of the stone columns of the Grounding. He had a large rock in his hand, which he was hefting experimentally.

I've learned a great deal from you Skin-Dwellers, Baasalt thought. He drew his arm back and launched the rock like a cannonball.

"Not enough," Angel grunted, and swung the bar from his shoulders. It connected solidly with the rock, sending it rocketing straight into the face of another Quake demon. The Tremblor staggered backward a few steps and collapsed.

"That's called a line drive," Angel said. "Good for a single. You want to try for a grand slam, I'm ready."

Rome laughed. "Not bad. A shame there's no place to run."

I suppose, Baasalt thought, *we'll have to do this the old-fashioned way, then.*

Another Tremblor charged. Angel concentrated on weak spots once more, and managed to drive the demon back. There was another one waiting right behind the first.

It went on and on. Angel couldn't even kill them, just hurt them enough to make them drop back— and be replaced by another.

He knew Baasalt was right. He couldn't keep this up forever.

His world contracted into a mindless rhythm of violence, of strikes and spins and lunges. His arms ached and his lungs burned, but he would not give up . . .

"Typical," a voice said. "Can't leave you alone for a few minutes without you gettin' in a fight."

The Tremblors paused and turned, as one. Doyle stood at the entrance to the cave with a satchel in his hand, and he wasn't alone. A group of Serpentene was gathered around him.

You were foolish to come here, Baasalt thought. *Here, we are powerful and you are weak. We will bury you all.*

Doyle shook his head. "I don't think so. Even here, you've got a weakness—'Only that which opposes you can oppose you,' right? Took me a long time t'figure out what that meant, but I think I finally did."

Doyle reached into the satchel and pulled something out. He lobbed it overhand at Angel and yelled, "Catch!" at the same time.

Angel snatched it out of the air one-handed, praying it was a weapon.

It was plastic. It was bright pink.

It was a hair-dryer.

"You've gotta be kidding," he groaned.

"Runs on batteries," Doyle said. "And dispenses the element opposite to earth—wind."

Angel understood in a flash. He thumbed the On switch—and shot the nearest Tremblor in the face with a blast of air.

The effect was instantaneous. The Quake demon's head came apart like a sandcastle in a windstorm, leaving only a skull that looked like it was made of crystal. The Tremblor collapsed, the skull ringing on the rock floor but not breaking.

"Now!" Doyle said.

He moved aside, revealing a bulky shape wrapped in a tarpaulin behind him, one that took up most of the tunnel. The Serpentene yanked the tarp off, revealing their secret weapon: a Hollywood wind machine, a giant portable fan.

The blades began to revolve . . . and the air in the cave began to move.

The reaction of the Tremblors was automatic and instinctive; they tried to escape. Since the cave's only exit was blocked, they tried to make their own, digging into the rocky walls or floor of the cave.

All except Baasalt.

No. I will not be defeated by the Void which Screams. I will not!

He picked up a chunk of rock and cocked his arm. Angel knew all it would take to disable the fan would be one hit on the blades.

He brought the hair-dryer up, and blasted hot air over Baasalt's pitching arm. The glossy black rock blew off like fine ash, leaving only the crystalline bone of the arm underneath. The rock fell from fingers like cut diamonds.

Baasalt had enough time to meet Angel's eyes.

But we are Eternal! Baasalt thought.

"You're dust," Angel said.

If the floor of the cave had been dirt, the Tremblors might have stood a chance; but they couldn't dig through the hard rock fast enough, even with their tremor-inducing abilities. The cave began to shake as two hundred frantic Quake demons tried to escape their fate—and failed.

An artificial wind blew through the cave as the fan pumped air. It scoured the rocky flesh from the Tremblors' bones, turning them into gemstone statues that stood for a frozen instant before tumbling to the ground with a glittering clatter. The air swirled with sparkling bits of obsidian.

Something smashed at Angel's feet: Baasalt's skull. Weakened by the hole the pickax had made, it had shattered when it hit the ground.

"Let's get these people out of here," Angel said. "I don't think this cavern is going to hold up much longer." He pointed to the six columns that had held the Grounding; there were big empty gaps in the middle of each of them now.

"What about him?" Doyle asked, jerking a thumb at Rome.

"I'll give you a thirty-second head start," Angel growled at the Associate. Rome said nothing, just nodded and slipped past the wind machine. Doyle and the Serpentene grabbed the three unconscious hostages and carried them out.

Angel took one last look around. The pickax

he'd planted in Baasalt's head was lying in the rubble of the First Warrior-Priest's jeweled bones. Angel leaned over and picked it up—then tossed it into the lava pit. The wooden handle burst into flames as the steel head sank into the molten rock.

CHAPTER THIRTEEN

"I can't believe it!" Cordelia exclaimed. "The office—it looks just the way it did before!"

"Yeah, they really did a bang-up job," Doyle said. He poured himself a cup of coffee. "Only took 'em a few days, too—"

"It's terrible! Angel, tell him it's terrible."

Angel looked up from the book he was reading. "It's . . . exactly the same," he said.

"Right! And what's the point in that? We could have had a brand-new office, with actual decor! This—this is like *anti*-decor. If this office and a real office met, there would be an explosion."

Angel put down his book and got to his feet. "I like the decor, anti or not. I asked Galvin to put it back just the way it was."

Cordelia sighed and threw her hands in the air.

"Why am I even bothering? I'm talking to the man who gives fashion tips to ninjas."

Doyle chuckled. "C'mon, Cordy. How can you be annoyed after depositing the bonus check the Serpentene gave us?"

Cordy frowned. "What bonus check?"

"Just remembered an important appointment," Angel said hastily. "Demons. Nasty. Gotta go."

Cordelia cut him off before he could reach the door. "Angel?" she said warningly. "*What* bonus check?"

"The . . . bonus check I haven't given you yet?"

"From the Serpentene? Why not? Are you afraid I'm going to run off to Acapulco or something?"

Angel looked uncomfortable. "Of course not. I'm just not satisfied that the case has been completely resolved."

"What he means," Doyle said, gesturing with his coffee cup, "is that we still don't know why Wolfram and Hart wanted the Serpentene's property, and Galvin never even brought it up. Nice of him to save Angel's bacon and all, but there's still somethin' screwy goin' on."

"Exactly," Angel said. "And until I know exactly what that is, I can't cash this check. Sorry."

"All right, all right," Cordelia said. "Can I just . . . look at it? Please?"

"I don't think that would be a good idea," Angel said, shaking his head.

"That much, huh?" Cordelia said sadly. "Oh, well. At least we still have our honor, yadda yadda yadda."

"It's more than some people have," Angel said.

Associate Rome sat in his office, in the dark, and waited for the end.

He had failed. Not only was the vampire still alive—or at least undead—but the Tremblors had been destroyed. His leverage with the Serpentene was gone.

The senior partners did not approve of failure.

He considered options. While he could no longer snap up the Serpentene property for a song, it was possible they still might deal with him—as long as they didn't realize the true value of what they sat on. It would just take more money . . .

He picked up his phone, and placed a call.

"One thing I still don't get," Cordelia said. "Wolfram and Hart were helping the Tremblors, and the Tremblors were going to cause this huge earthquake that would destroy L.A., which is where Wolfram and Hart have their big shiny office tower headquarters. Why would they do that?"

Lisbon rose up in Angel's mind once more; the fires, the looting, the rats. Him and Darla, playing in the ruins . . . "Any huge natural disaster attracts scavengers," Angel said. "Opportunists who prey on the victims. Black marketeers, real estate speculators—even thrill-seekers. There are a hundred different ways to profit from large-scale human suffering, and I'm sure Wolfram and Hart knows them all. If the quake had happened, I'm betting the W & H tower would have been one of the few buildings left standing."

"Which still doesn't answer what they wanted the Serpentene's property for," Doyle said.

"Actually, I've had some ideas of my own about that," Angel said.

"Oh?" Doyle said. "Like what?"

"I'd rather run them past Galvin first," Angel said. "As a matter of fact, I'm heading over there now. And Cordelia—if I'm wrong, we'll cash that check, I promise."

Angel shrugged on his trenchcoat as he headed out the door.

"Well, there goes the rent," Cordelia said. She picked up a watering can and started watering the office plants.

"Maybe not," Doyle said. "He did say he might be wrong—"

"He's not wrong," Cordelia said. "He's Angel. I'm still amazed you figured out that whole Tremblor-wind thing before he did."

"Well, he was kinda busy being held captive in

the bowels of the Earth," Doyle said. "But give me a *little* credit, willya?"

"Why?"

"Why? Well, I did sorta save the day, right?"

Cordelia rolled her eyes. "Doyle, *please*. Galvin supplied the equipment, the Serpentene did most of the work and Angel did the fighting. All you did was make a lucky guess."

"Not true. I figured it out honestly."

"How?"

"Well, it was our prisoner that clued me in. When Angel was threatenin' to expose him t'the big blue sky, the Tremblor coulda just closed his eyes, but he was still terrified. That's because any little breeze would have turned him into a dust cloud. T'them, the Void wasn't just empty space—it was space filled with an invisible, untouchable enemy."

"That's obvious, now, Doyle, but this could all be twenty-twenty hindsight. I was there, remember? You just thought they were dumb."

"Okay, okay, it didn't click all at once, but I'll tell you the kicker. Vampires and running water."

"You were inspired while using Angel's bathroom?"

"No, no. It's one of those myths about vamps that gets Angel so hacked off. That's probably the reason he didn't figure it out first; he's got a mental block when it comes t'these things. Anyway, people used t'say that a vampire couldn't cross running water, or even that falling into running water would destroy them. It was one small leap from vamps and movin' water to demons and movin' air."

"So your reasoning was based on something that wasn't true."

"Well, there was a certain element o' speculation—"

"Like I said. You guessed."

Doyle shrugged and changed the subject. "So, how are you and Maureen gettin' on? Still best buds?"

Cordelia put down the watering can. "Actually, I haven't heard from her since the whole rescue thing. I think she's pretty busy, what with her place getting trashed and all."

"Sure."

Cordelia frowned. "What, you don't think she'll want to hang with me now that the case has been solved?"

"Guess we'll see. But don't worry, Cordy, you can always hang with me."

"That's sweet, Doyle, but a day at the racetrack is not my idea of a good time."

Doyle did his best to look hurt. "Racetrack? Is that the only place you think I'm familiar with?"

"Of course not. I'm sure you could give me an extensive tour of topless bars, too."

"How about the Griffith Observatory?"

"What?"

"The Griffith Observatory. Big white building on a hill with a telescope sticking out of the roof."

"I know what the Griffith Observatory is, Doyle. I just never figured *you* would."

"It's kinda interestin', actually. I know you haven't been in L.A. all that long, and you probably haven't seen it yet. If you ever want to check it out, let me know. I'll play tour guide."

Cordelia studied him for a moment, then smiled. "Well, I was never into the whole science thing, but I do hear they use it for location shoots a lot. Thanks. I'll keep that in mind."

Doyle smiled back, then got himself another cup of coffee so she wouldn't see the smile turn into a grin.

"Good to see you again, Angel," Galvin said, clapping him on the shoulder as he walked through the door. "Satisfied with the repairs, I hope?"

"They're fine," Angel said.

He followed Galvin into the living room and sat down. Galvin's expensive furnishings had been replaced by cheap knockoffs; the tunnel entrance had been boarded over with plywood.

"I see you haven't renovated yet," Angel said.

"No. I decided to use this as an excuse to redecorate, and I haven't quite decided on a theme yet."

"How about 'Deception'?"

Galvin looked at Angel for a second, his smile frozen on his face. "Pardon me?"

"Or maybe that isn't quite accurate," Angel continued. "How about 'Manipulation'? Or even good old-fashioned 'Greed'?"

"I don't understand."

"Sure you do. Does the name Rudolpho Faranetti ring a bell?"

"Ah. Icepick Rudy. I see you've been doing some checking around." Galvin nodded his head.

"That I have. What I found out was that Faranetti got into a lot of trouble with his employers— seemed he'd leaked certain secrets he shouldn't have. Thing was, he didn't leak them to the police; he leaked them to you."

"I suppose it would be pointless to deny it," Galvin said. He strolled over to a cheap wooden cabinet and opened it up, revealing a bar. "Care for a drink?"

"No thanks. I don't think I like the prices you charge."

"We charge whatever the market will bear. Isn't that the idea behind capitalism? We offered Mr. Faranetti something he very much wanted, and we asked for something equally valuable in return. He could have said no."

"And you used the information to blackmail the Corzato crime family. What do they give you, ten percent of whatever they make?"

"It's more in the nature of a flat fee in their case—their accounting is atrocious." Galvin poured a shot of brandy into a glass. "But it's hardly exorbitant."

"Because, of course, they're not the first—or only—people you extort," Angel said. "You've got a room full of people's dreams, all neatly labeled."

Galvin chuckled and sat down across from Angel. "You have been thorough; I should have expected that. Yes, the Serpentene have a talent for discovering those things that mean the most to people, things now lost—or even things that were never more than dreams in the first place. A picture of a parent you never got to meet. A stuffed toy that kept you sane through a childhood of abuse. Even a movie never filmed, a book never written: we have an excellent print of *The Wizard of Oz* starring Orson Welles as the Cowardly Lion."

"I'm sure it's fascinating—but hardly worth selling your soul for."

Galvin laughed. "Quite right! And we don't deal in souls, Angel—we're not that kind of demon. We're more niche marketers."

"You deal in secrets."

"Precisely. We give people what they want, in return for sensitive information: stock tips, investment opportunities—"

"Blackmail information."

"We prefer to think of it as preferential negotiation." Galvin took a sip of his brandy. "We're just doing what snakes do naturally, Angel; once we're wrapped around someone . . . we *squeeze*."

Angel shook his head. "How do you do it? Where do you get this stuff?"

"Alternate realities. I won't divulge details about how we obtain the items, but suffice it to say that for every reality where a treasured item was lost, there is another where it wasn't."

"You trade people's dreams for other people's dirty laundry. No wonder you like it down here; you belong under a rock."

"I'm sorry you see it that way," Galvin sighed.

"You know I can't let you keep on doing this."

"What are you going to do? Kill us all? And our children, too?"

Angel said nothing.

"What we do isn't so different from what everyone in L.A. does," Galvin said. "We give people their dreams. And we exact a high price from those too weak to resist temptation."

"This town has enough people like you already,"

Angel said darkly. "Maybe you should think about relocating. Before *I* decide to squeeze *you.*"

"I see your point. Perhaps it's time to move on; we *have* had an offer on the building—"

"—which you intended to sell all along."

"Ah. I keep forgetting you're a detective. I see you know about our negotiations with Wolfram and Hart."

"Is that what this was all about? Negotiations?"

"One must always negotiate from a position of strength, particularly when dealing with a powerful opponent. We thank you; eliminating the Quake demons raised Wolfram and Hart's offer considerably."

Angel reached into his pocket and pulled out the check the Serpentene had given him. He handed it to Galvin. "I can't accept this."

"Why not? It's perfectly good, I assure you."

"You and I have different definitions of 'good.'"

Galvin shrugged and took the check. "Suit yourself."

"One more thing. Why do Wolfram and Hart want this property so bad?"

Galvin smiled. "Emilio Maldonado."

"Never heard of him."

"He's a geologist who lost his son a few years ago. At least, that's what happened in this reality; in another, it was Emilio who died and his son who grieved. We arranged an introduction between the two; each fills the other's needs. Emilio has a very different view of us than you do. To him, we're saviors."

"Until it's time to pay the price. What did he do for you in return?"

"He convinced Wolfram and Hart that this property was a great deal more valuable than it would seem to be. As a result, they are now willing to pay us a great deal of money, far more than its actual value. 'The enemy of my enemy is my friend'—I'm sure you've heard that before? Well, Wolfram and Hart will shortly have good reason to hate us both— doesn't that make you happy?"

"Be glad it doesn't. And while I approve of anything that puts a crimp in Wolfram and Hart's plans, what happens to Maldonado when they find out?"

"I believe that falls into your area, not ours. 'Helping the helpless'—correct?"

"I'll do what I can."

"I'm sure you will. Associate Rome, however . . . something tells me he's on his own."

"If you take his bosses for as much money as I think you will, Associate Rome will wish he'd never been spawned."

Galvin put his hands behind his head. "Oh, the

amount will be considerable; you can trust me on that."

"Just what do they think they're getting?"

"A massive deposit of crude oil."

"Right," Angel said. "Snake oil . . ."

Galvin grinned.

And despite himself, Angel laughed.

About the Author

Don DeBrandt writes science fiction, fantasy, horror, superheroes, cyberpunk, cyberfolk, and cyberanything else. Spider Robinson has compared DeBrandt's fiction to that of Larry Niven and John Varley; his first novel, *The Quicksilver Screen*, made *Locus* magazine's recommended reading list for 1992. He's also published horror fiction in *Pulphouse*, and a novella in the SF magazine *Horizons*. His fiction has earned him Honorable Mentions in both the *Year's Best SF* and the *Year's Best Fantasy and Horror*.

He was written two stage plays for high schools, *Heart of Glass* and *Happy Hour at the Secret Hideout*, and has worked as a freelancer for Marvel Comics on such titles as *Spiderman 2099* and *2099 Unlimited*. His other comics work include several stories for the anthology comic *Freeflight*. He has short stories in all three volumes of the *Deadlands* gaming anthology.

DeBrandt lives in Burnaby, B.C. His hobbies include leather-tasting, naked laughing gas hot tubbing, stilting, and being thrown off roofs by irate hotel security. Despite rumors to the contrary, he does not have an evil twin. *There are no such things as evil twins.*

"Wish me monsters."
—Buffy

Vampires, werewolves, witches, demons of nonspecific origin. All of them are drawn to the Hellmouth in Sunnydale, California. And all of them have met their fate at the hands—or stake—of Buffy the Vampire Slayer.

This volume catalogs and explores the mythological, literary, and cultural origins of the endless numbers of ghoulish creatures who have tried to take a piece of the Slayer in the first four years of the hit TV show.

Buffy
the vampire slayer™

THE MONSTER BOOK
by
Christopher Golden
Stephen R. Bissette
Thomas E. Sniegoski

AVAILABLE NOW FROM

POCKET BOOKS

Buffy
the vampire slayer™

SPIKE AND DRU:
PRETTY MAIDS ALL IN A ROW

The year is 1940.

In exchange for a powerful jewel, Spike and Drusilla agree to kill the current Slayer—and all those targeted to succeed her. If they succeed with their plans of bloodlust and power, it could mean the end of the Chosen One—*all* of the Chosen Ones—forever....

A *Buffy* hardcover
by Christopher Golden

Available from Pocket Books

... A GIRL BORN
WITHOUT THE FEAR GENE

FEARLESS™

A SERIES BY
FRANCINE PASCAL

POCKET
PULSE

**FROM POCKET PULSE
PUBLISHED BY POCKET BOOKS**

3029